Joel peeled open a candy bar and held it out to Amy, apparently oblivious to the fact that she had just repeatedly rejected him.

Amy pushed it away. "You know what? You've got to go now. I'm calling Ephram. Most nights we fall asleep on the phone, so there's no point in waiting." Amy hit her speed dial. Ephram's name came up on her cell's screen. She smiled at it.

"Ephram's phone," a girl said in her ear. "Zoe here. Speak to me."

Shocked, Amy hit the END button. She stared at the phone as if it were some sort of poisonous creature.

"Nice." The Grin made its biggest appearance yet. "A girl just answered your boyfriend's phone."

Joel knew a great exit line, and he used it, leaving Amy alone to hear that girl's voice in her head over and over again.

EVERWOOD

Making Choices

By Laura J. Burns and Melinda Metz
Based on the television series created by Greg Berlanti

SIMON SPOTLIGHT ENTERTAINMENT
New York London Toronto Sydney

If you purchased this book without a cover, you should be aware that this book is stolen property. It was reported as "unsold and destroyed" to the publisher, and neither the author nor the publisher has received any payment for this "stripped book."

This book is a work of fiction. Any references to historical events, real people, or real locales are used fictitiously. Other names, characters, places, and incidents are the product of the author's imagination, and any resemblance to actual events or locales or persons, living or dead, is entirely coincidental.

SSE

SIMON SPOTLIGHT ENTERTAINMENT
An imprint of Simon & Schuster Children's Publishing Division
1230 Avenue of the Americas, New York, New York 10020

Manufactured in the United States of America
First Edition 10 9 8 7 6 5 4 3 2 1
Library of Congress Control Number 2004102538
ISBN 0-689-87108-2

EVERWOOD

Making Choices

PROLOGUE

Ephram Brown took a deep breath of the clear Colorado air and smiled in spite of himself. As much as he had tried to hate Everwood, he had to admit that his inborn New Yorker's disdain for nature was seriously starting to fade. How could anyone not love the taste of that pollution-free air, the feel of the warm sun on one's skin?

And suddenly the sensations were rushing at him all at once: his hands, not frozen onto the handlebars of his bike; ears, not throbbing with the pain of impending frostbite; his breath, not making clouds in the air. For the first time in months, he could hear his bike's tires crunching over gravel without a slush puddle in sight. "I'm hot," he murmured aloud. He twisted around, pulling off his jacket as he kept one hand on the handlebars.

There was no denying it: Summer had arrived.

The familiar dizzying feeling of anticipation began making its way up from his stomach. Three more days of school, and then freedom. Summer, the best time of the year. Especially *this* year. Because this year he was going to spend the summer studying piano at Juilliard. Juilliard, the best music school in the world, in the best city in the world—New York City—where there would be nothing but piano all summer long: no father to annoy him, no little sister to pester him, and most important, nothing to remind him of Madison.

Just the thought of her made Ephram pedal slower. He waited for the usual dull ache in his throat, the feeling that he couldn't get enough air into his lungs—the pain, the embarrassment, the misery. But it didn't come. There was just a sort of emptiness, a lack of emotion.

"Huh," he muttered. Hadn't been expecting *that*. After all, Madison's very existence had been torturing him for months: first when he hated her; then later when she was his girlfriend and he couldn't stop wanting to touch her, to breathe her in, to just stare at her all day long and dream of her all night; and, of course, when she broke his heart. Somehow the pain of the breakup seemed to linger on a lot longer than the happiness of being with her. And looking back, Ephram had to admit that the pain of losing Madison had been as deep as the love he'd felt for her. In fact the pain just might have been deeper.

He shuddered in the warm air as he thought of those first few days after their breakup. The overwhelming hurt had been worse than anything he'd felt in his life—except, of course, when he lost his mom. Ephram had kind of thought that he had a get-out-of-jail-free card when it came to grieving. Nothing could be worse than his mom dying. It just never occurred to him that other kinds of loss would hurt too. He hadn't even wanted to get out of bed after Madison dumped him. And he might have just stayed under the covers if his father hadn't been there.

You had to hand it to the guy: Dr. Andy Brown had come a long way in the past two years. For most of Ephram's life he'd been nothing more than the self-satisfied windbag who occasionally ate dinner with them. It was Julia, Ephram's mom, who did all the actual parenting. But since her death, Ephram's father had really stepped up. Even though he'd never approved of Ephram's relationship with Madison, he didn't say "I told you so" when they broke up. Instead he spent hours just sitting in Ephram's room, sometimes talking, sometimes being silent—but always appreciated.

It had taken a while, but Ephram could finally admit that he loved his dad. When he most needed a parent, his father had been there for him. And that almost made the pain of losing Madison bearable. Well, that and the fact that Delia had fired

Madison as her baby-sitter. It was truly a lifesaver not to have to see his ex-girlfriend in his living room every day.

The memory of Madison still had the power to plunge him right back into misery, but this crystal clear early summer day was too beautiful to waste being miserable. "Juilliard summer program," Ephram said aloud, forcing his mind away from his ex and back to what was important: the future—*his* future—as a musician.

For as long as he could remember, Ephram had loved the piano. In fact he couldn't even remember a time when he didn't know how to play. The feeling of the keys under his fingers was as natural as breathing. Taking lessons, practicing, and giving recitals had always seemed easy, even relaxing. It was just another part of who he was.

Until his mother died.

Ephram hadn't played for months after the car accident that took her away from them. And when he finally started again, things had changed. He could still play, of course, but it wasn't easy anymore. It was as if Ephram had something to prove, something he had to say through his music. And that made it harder. How could you enjoy playing when you were suddenly aware of how much it meant to you, when you felt your dead mother's presence every time you sat down at the piano?

To make everything even more difficult, everyone was talking about college. Amy Abbott, his first true love, had been the one to bring it up. He'd sat in the gym bleachers with Amy as their fathers tore through the college information fair. All Ephram had wanted to do was take in Amy's long, beautiful hair and her big brown eyes, but she'd kept going on about college—how they had to think of their futures, and how their parents and teachers were going to be focused on college applications and the SAT from then forward. Amy hadn't seemed too happy about any of it. But for Ephram, the college issue brought up even deeper feelings of panic. He'd always assumed that he would go to Juilliard. That's what talented pianists did in New York. You grew up taking lessons, you gave recitals and built up a reputation, and then you went to Juilliard.

It had hit Ephram like a sucker punch. He'd never given a single thought to college, but he'd never realized that he'd been counting on Juilliard his whole life. And here he was in Everwood, Colorado, far from the concert stages of New York and completely out of practice. And after playing—badly—for the visiting Juilliard professor, it was painfully clear that it was going to take a miracle for him to get in. A miracle, or a last resort.

Putting himself in front of more Juilliard professors to audition for the summer program . . . well, let's just say he'd almost needed a fresh set of boxers. But he had dragged himself out onto that stage, looked at Amy, and played. And he'd gotten in! He leaned forward, pedaling faster in preparation for the last big hill before home. Adrenaline surged through his veins as he thought about his summer. It was his chance to make up for slacking off since he moved to Everwood, his chance to prove to Juilliard and the other great conservatories that he was good enough. Professors from everywhere would come to the final concert.

And he *was* good enough. Ephram had to believe that. His mother had thought he was good enough, and his teacher in Everwood, Will Cleveland, thought so too. And those were the two people in the world whose opinions Ephram trusted. He was good enough. He'd made the first cut. Now he had to go all the way and earn himself a spot at Juilliard once he graduated from high school.

As he crested the hill he stopped pedaling and coasted down the other side toward home. The warm wind whipped through his hair and the sun was so bright it practically blinded him. Ephram didn't mind. There was never any traffic on this street, and he felt like for far too long, he hadn't let himself be dazzled by the sunshine. The winters were long in Colorado. He felt the bump under his tires that indicated the pavement in front of Nina's, the house next door to his. With a happy sigh,

Ephram braked and turned into his driveway, squinting into the sun.

Someone was sitting on the steps that led up to the front porch. Ephram parked his bike and climbed off, black spots still swimming in his vision from the bright light.

"Delia?" he called. His little sister usually got home from school before him. Maybe she was locked out.

"Um, not exactly."

He stopped, stunned. His vision was finally clearing, but he didn't need to see to know who'd spoken. He recognized the voice instantly: Amy.

Ephram felt a heat in his face that had nothing to do with the sun. What was Amy doing here? Wasn't she still pissed at him? When she'd found out that her brother had told Ephram that Amy liked him—more than liked him—but Ephram hadn't let on to Amy that he knew, she'd felt humiliated. And betrayed. And pissed.

He'd tried to remind her of the times she'd lied by omission to him—like when she basically broke his heart because she wanted the Great Dr. Brown to perform surgery on Colin Hart, her boyfriend who was in a coma. But Amy hadn't exactly seen it that way.

"Hey," Ephram said stupidly. He walked slowly toward the house as Amy climbed to her feet. God, she was beautiful. The memory of their kiss came rushing back as he looked at her, that one kiss before everything went to crap. He'd just been soaking in the warmth of her skin, the softness of her lips on his, the feeling that they should've been doing this sort of thing for years already. He'd loved Amy since the first time he saw her. He knew that part of him would always love her. Then Amy was asking him why he hadn't been more surprised when she told him that she liked him. . . .

"Hey, Ephram." Her tone was as sweet and musical as ever.

Danger! shouted a little voice in Ephram's mind. *Beware the Amy Vortex!*

"What are you doing here?" he blurted out. It sounded rude, like he didn't want her there, like she shouldn't have come, but maybe that was the truth. The Amy Vortex was a real place, and Ephram had been trapped there for an entire year. He was all too familiar with the feeling of being crushed by Amy's "friendship." He had spent months being devoted to her, in love with her, completely and utterly dedicated to what was best for Amy . . . and in return all he'd gotten was the occasional hint that someday, *maybe*, she would change her mind and love him back. Now, true, she'd admitted that she "more than liked him." But she could be back here with a different story. She could need time. She might think they needed to work on the friend part. And even if she was going to actually tell him again—well, not quite tell him—that she *really* liked him, they'd already proved they couldn't be with each other for one whole day without Vortex time.

Ephram was not going back to that place. It didn't matter how amazing their kiss had been. It didn't matter that Amy knew him better and made him laugh harder than anyone else, even Madison. Nothing mattered except his own future. Ephram took a deep breath and gave himself an instant mantra: Juilliard. Not Amy. Nothing but Juilliard. *Juilliard,* he thought, trying to ignore Amy's hurt puppy-dog eyes. *Juilliard.*

"Look, maybe I shouldn't have come," Amy said. "I know we haven't exactly been close lately."

Juilliard, Ephram thought.

"I just . . . I miss you," she went on. "A lot."

Ephram swallowed down the lump in his throat. *Juilliard.*

"And I know this is probably the last thing you want," Amy added. "But I just have to know one thing. I mean, I just have to ask or I'll regret it."

Ephram nodded. *Juilliard.*

"Will you go out with me?" Amy asked. "On a date?"

"Absolutely," Ephram answered without hesitating for a second.

CHAPTER 1

"Revenge of the cowlick," Ephram muttered. He'd been staring at himself in the mirror for at least ten minutes now, hands slathered in hair gel, eyes filled with desperation. He was supposed to pick up Amy in fifteen minutes. That left him exactly thirty seconds to calm his insane hair, brush his teeth, choose the perfect outfit, go to the store, and buy some roses before heading over to the Abbott house.

He massaged some more sticky hair products onto his stubborn cowlick. It remained standing upright, and now it sort of gleamed from all the gunk he'd put on it. Meanwhile the rest of his hair just looked greasy and lay flat, plastered to his head.

"Screw it," he growled, slamming the tube down onto the bathroom counter. In a fury, he turned the water on full-force and stuck his head into the sink. His hair was so covered in goo that the water just ran off it as if he were waterproof.

"Need some help?" His dad's voice was muffled by the running water, but Ephram could still hear the tone of amusement. *Smug jerk,* he thought. He decided to ignore his father's presence in the bathroom and concentrate on wetting down his hair. He stuck his fingers in and scrubbed as hard as he could, splashing water all over the counter.

"Whoa!" his dad cried. "I think you've done enough." He reached over Ephram's head and turned off the faucet.

Ephram stood up and shook his head like a dog. His father laughed outright.

"What?" Ephram turned to look in the mirror. Behind the splatters of water, the image of Ephram the Troll Doll gazed back at him. The cowlick was still standing straight up, but it was hard to tell—all the other hair on his head was standing straight up too.

"Crap," Ephram muttered, flattening his hair with his wet hands. "Crap, crap, crap."

"Nice language," his father commented.

"Now is not the time," Ephram warned him. "I'm late and I look like I just took a swim in the Hudson."

"You look fine," his dad said.

"Really?"

"Sure."

Ephram looked back into the mirror. His hair was mostly where it should be now. Maybe he could get away with it.

"You should just push down that cowlick," his dad added, reaching over to flatten the offending hair.

Ephram's face grew hot. "Don't touch me," he snapped. He pushed past his father and headed down the hall. His stupid hair would just have to look bad. Maybe he could wear a baseball cap.

To his horror, his father followed him to his room. "Big date, huh?" he asked.

"The biggest," Ephram said. He began searching on his floor for his favorite pair of jeans. He liked to leave them on the rug near the dresser after he'd worn them. They always looked best on the second wearing after being washed—one wearing loosened them up, and the next time he wore them they were perfect. He'd purposely worn them to school the other day to break them in for tonight. So where were they?

"You know, Ephram, you and Amy have a . . . well, a complicated history," his father began.

"Yeah, so?" Ephram lifted up the bedspread and peered underneath. Where were his jeans?

"So you might want to tread carefully here," his dad went on. "Amy has hurt you before. And you're just getting over being hurt by Madison—"

"Dad, please. No lectures," Ephram interrupted. "Just help me find my jeans. I'm incredibly late."

"The jeans you left on the floor?"

Ephram stopped searching and turned to his father. "Why do you know that?" he demanded.

"I put them in the laundry," his dad said innocently. "They're not dry yet, though."

"Dad!" Ephram yelled.

"What? You threw them on the floor, I assumed they were dirty."

"Unbelievable." Ephram turned to his closet and began searching for another acceptable pair of pants. "The one time in history you decide to do laundry, you manage to ruin my first date with Amy."

"Are you telling me that a pair of jeans is the key to a successful romantic relationship?" his dad asked.

"We'll never know now, will we?" Ephram grabbed a pair of too-blue, too-tight jeans off the shelf in his closet. He glared at his dad for good measure. "Do you mind?"

"Okay, okay, I'll leave." His father headed toward the bedroom door. "Just don't stay out too late. Oh, and, Ephram?"

Ephram rolled his eyes. "What now?"

"Remember, Amy's your friend," his dad said. "She doesn't care what your hair looks like or which pants you're wearing. She already likes you."

Ephram watched him go. That was the thing about Dr. Andy Brown. Sometimes—but only occasionally—he knew the right thing to say.

Is her father going to answer the door? Ephram wondered as he drove. He knew Dr. Abbott had never liked him. Although really, compared to Amy's drug-dealing ex-boyfriend, he should come off pretty well. But what if it wasn't her father? What if Bright answered the door? Ephram knew his friend well enough to be certain that the bullying frat boy at the center of Bright's soul wouldn't be able to pass up a chance to mock him for wearing the ugly jeans on a date. And Bright was not above teasing Ephram in front of Amy.

"Please let it be her mother," Ephram whispered as he turned into the Abbott driveway. He just couldn't face any further stress before the date officially started. It was hard enough knowing that he was about to have another shot with the girl of his dreams—probably his last shot. The pressure was almost unbearable. What if he blew it? What if he somehow screwed things up again? What if Amy took one look at him and thought, "What am I doing with this complete geek?"

Ephram climbed out of the car and made his way to the front door, trying to ignore the sick feeling in his stomach. He really should've bought the roses earlier today—that way he would at least have something to hide behind. As it was, he hadn't had time to stop at the store. Now he couldn't figure out what to do with his hands. He rang the bell, then clasped his hands together behind his back. That looked manly, right?

The door opened so fast that he took a step backward in surprise.

"Let's go," Amy said, rushing past him and heading for the car.

"Okay. . . ." Ephram took off after her and managed to get to her car door right as she opened it for herself. She looked at him questioningly.

"Um, just trying to be a gentleman," he muttered. "I suck at it."

Amy grinned and got into the car. Ephram closed the door for her and ran around to his side. As he pulled out, Amy sighed in relief. "I was afraid my dad or Bright would answer the door," she said. "I'd never hear the end of it. Just a little too much pressure for our first date, you know? I guess last time was a date, really. But let's not count it. It was spontaneous. Not planned. No picking up at the house. So it doesn't have to count."

And right then and there, Ephram knew that this was going to be the best date of his life. "This is definitely our first," he agreed.

The movie wasn't funny even though it was supposed to be. And the pizza they got afterward was bad, just like all pizza outside of New York.

But Ephram had never had a better time watching a bad film and eating soggy pizza. How could this date be anything *but* amazing? He was with Amy, who was pretty much his best friend, not to mention the most beautiful, amazing girl he'd ever known. Back when they'd first met, when she was still worrying about Colin, Ephram had been the only one who could make her laugh. And miraculously, he hadn't lost that. He and Amy had both had a rough year, and there were times when he hadn't been sure that either of them would ever laugh again. But all evening long, they laughed so hard that they could hardly catch their breath. It felt like the sudden coming of summer—an unexpected release from the long, cold, miserable year.

After dinner, Ephram didn't want to go home. He didn't want Amy to go home either. But he didn't have much choice in the matter. When he was with Madison, they would go to the Point and make out. But it was way too soon to ask Amy to go there with him. In fact Ephram couldn't even make his brain go too far in that direction. Just the fact that Amy Abbott was here on a date with him was more than he could comprehend. The physical stuff had nothing to do with it. Well, almost nothing—at least for right now.

So he drove her home. Not too late, just like his father had said. He parked in front of the Abbott house and turned off the ignition. From inside came the glow of a lamp, and Ephram knew without a doubt that Dr. Abbott was right inside, listening for the car, and waiting for Ephram to leave.

"So I guess I should go," he said.

"Yeah, my dad's a little overprotective since the whole Tommy thing," Amy said. "I probably shouldn't blame him."

Ephram reached for her hand. Tommy had been bad news, a drug abuser and a dealer. But he knew that Amy had cared about the guy. She had wanted to help him, and the breakup hit her hard.

She squeezed his hand gratefully. "I'm glad I can talk about that with you," she said. "You don't freak out when I say his name. You're the only one."

"I get it," Ephram said. "You saw the potential in him and you wanted to help him realize it. Just like you saw the potential coolness in a dweeb like me when we first met."

Amy gave him a little punch with their joined hands. "And maybe someday you'll actually achieve coolness, Ephram. I believe in you."

"Nice." Ephram smiled. Being teased by Amy was one of his favorite things.

"Okay, so . . ."

"I'll walk you to the door," Ephram said. "Stay there."

"You *are* being a gentleman tonight," Amy said

with a grin. She sat in her seat until he made it around the car to open her door.

"It's all a show in case your dad is watching through the curtains," he told her, helping her out.

The walk to the front door was way too short, even though he held Amy's hand the entire way. At the door she turned to him, her brown eyes nervous.

"What's wrong?" he asked.

"I'm not sure how this will work," she told him.

"How *what* will work?"

In answer, Amy leaned in and kissed him. Her lips were impossibly soft, and the kiss was so gentle that it took Ephram a moment to respond.

Amy pulled away and gazed up at him. "I guess that worked okay."

Ephram twined his hand in her thick hair and pulled her face back toward him for another kiss, this time not so gentle. He felt her arms slide around his back, her mouth moving under his. There was nothing in the world but Amy, this moment, this kiss.

She stepped back, breaking their contact. For a few seconds they just stared at one another, dazed. Then she gave him her trademark lopsided smile and opened the door. "Good night, Ephram."

"So how was it?" his father asked, the second Ephram walked in the door. Dr. Brown lay sprawled on the couch with a huge medical book splayed across his stomach. Ephram suspected that he'd been napping.

"Fine." Ephram headed for the stairs.

"Fine?" his father repeated indignantly. "I wait up all night for you and all I get is *fine*?"

"Dad, it's only eleven o'clock," Ephram pointed out. "I'd hardly call that 'all night.'"

"But—"

"G'night!" Ephram bounded up the stairs to his room. It was nice of his father to show an interest, but Ephram just wanted to be alone with his thoughts. He was on an Amy high, and he didn't want to share it with anyone.

But his dad was persistent. The next morning when Ephram went down to breakfast, his father was sitting at the counter, coffee in hand, clearly waiting to talk. Ephram ignored him.

Finally his dad couldn't take it anymore. "Well?" he demanded.

"Well . . ." Ephram smiled at the memory. "It was incredible. Amazing. Perfect. The best night of my life."

And he actually thought his father would be happy for him.

"Oh." That was all Dr. Brown said. Then he cleared his throat, the way he always did before he started on a lecture.

Uh-oh, Ephram thought. He looked around for a way to get out of the upcoming conversation, but his father had blocked the kitchen door.

"Ephram, you know I like Amy," Dr. Brown said.

Ephram was too surprised to answer. Amy? The speech was going to be about Amy? He thought his father was okay with Amy.

"But I've learned my lesson," his dad went on. "I didn't want you dating Madison because I was afraid you were going to get hurt. And it turned out I knew what I was talking about, so this time I'm going to do it right."

"This is a totally different situation," Ephram shot back. "Amy's my age! And she doesn't work for you! There's nothing even inappropriate about it."

"I know all that," his father replied. "Of course there's nothing wrong with you dating Amy—"

"Then what's your problem?" Ephram couldn't believe his dad was going to ruin this for him.

"Listen, I'm only trying to do what's best for you."

Ephram rolled his eyes. His mother would never have used such a cliché. "Amy is what's best for me," he said, "so there's no problem."

"I saw you with Madison, remember?" his dad continued. "I remember how in love with her you were."

"Not like this." Ephram was surprised to hear

himself say that, but as soon as the words left his mouth he realized they were true. And just like that, he was over Madison. One hundred percent, totally-and-forever *over* her. Because he was in love with Amy.

He had to see her. Right away. Not that he was going to run over there and blurt out that he loved her—he'd learned that lesson with Madison. But still, he needed to see her. Now. "I gotta go," he muttered, pushing past his father.

"No." It was a tone of voice Ephram had never heard before. His dad usually tried to be reasonable, to act like everybody's best pal. But this wasn't a friendly, how-ya-doin' tone. This was *parental.* Ephram froze.

"I'm sorry, Ephram, but I'm going to have to put my foot down," his father said. "I know how much you've always cared for Amy. But right now, your main focus has to be on your future. You're about to be a senior in high school."

"In three months," Ephram pointed out, turning back to face his dad. "I think I have time for a few dates."

"You insisted that you wanted to do this summer program," his father said. "Your dream is to get into Juilliard when you graduate—"

"Yeah, I know. It's *my* dream," Ephram interrupted.

"And it's my job to help you realize your dream.

That means buckling down and practicing." Dr. Brown stood up to emphasize his point. "Practicing every day. All the time. Living and breathing piano. That's what you said you wanted. That's why Will thought the program would be good for you."

"I will practice," Ephram said, "whenever I'm not with Amy."

"That's not good enough," his father replied. "I know how distracted you can get by your love life. You won't be able to do both."

Ephram felt hot from head to toe. *Distracted?* He had never witnessed such hypocrisy in his life. "Excuse me, you think *I* get distracted?" he sputtered. "You mean the way you were distracted by your career for the first fifteen years of my life?"

"That's different—"

"No, it's not!" Ephram cried. "And Amy isn't a distraction. She's a person. What do you think I'm gonna do, just pretend she doesn't exist? Act like I don't care about her and then I'll be all free to focus on piano?"

"You can't be with Amy and also be in New York," his father said. "I'm sorry, Ephram. You have to choose."

CHAPTER 2

"So what did you say?" Bright asked. Ephram was relieved that his friend had gotten over the need to tease him about Amy every single second. After three dates Bright had decided that the fun in that was gone. Now he was back to just being Ephram's friend. Not that Ephram felt entirely comfortable discussing Amy with her own brother. But the unreasonable Dr. Brown? *That* he could discuss.

"I told him to bite me," Ephram said.

"There is no way in hell you said that to your father."

"Okay, fine. I just ignored him. I've been ignoring him for a week now."

Bright shifted his weight and leaned back against Ephram's car. Ephram still didn't want to venture inside the Abbott house to pick up Amy. Dr. Abbott was too much to handle so early in their relationship.

Luckily Bright was always willing to come outside and keep him company while Amy got ready. "He has a point, you know," Bright said. "You're going away for the summer. It's not like you and Amy can have some great romance when you're a hundred miles from here."

"Two thousand miles," Ephram said.

Bright rolled his eyes. "Same difference."

The front door of the Abbott house slammed shut and Amy came bouncing down the front steps. All thoughts of his father vanished from Ephram's mind when he looked at Amy. The only thing he could think about was her. "Hey," she said cheerfully, giving him a quick kiss.

Somewhere in the background Bright snorted. Ephram was too busy being happy to care.

"So where are we going?" she asked.

"Straight to PDA-ville," Bright muttered. "I'm outta here."

Amy paid no attention to her brother, so Ephram ignored him too. "It's a surprise," he told Amy, pulling open the car door for her. He'd gotten better at that over the course of their last few dates. Amy slipped into the seat and waited while he came around to the driver's side. As they pulled away from the curb, she slipped her hand into his.

They held hands all night—on the drive over to the next town, where a traveling circus had set up their big top; through the clowns' and elephants' performances, which Amy pronounced scary and cute, respectively; while strolling around on the sawdust-laden grounds to watch the kids taking pony rides; and all the way back to Everwood. Ephram had never realized how important hand-holding could be, but right then it made him feel even more connected to Amy than he already did.

In fact he was so thrilled by their constant touching that it took him almost the entire drive home to notice that Amy wasn't saying anything. She held tightly to his hand, but stared out her window as if she were lost in thought.

He squeezed her hand. "Whatcha thinking?"

She turned her sad brown eyes toward him. "You leave in two days."

Ephram was so shocked he almost drove off the road. *Two days?* That couldn't be right. He quickly ran back over the past two weeks in his mind. School ended, he and Amy started dating. . . . It had all been such a happy blur that he hadn't even been paying attention to the calendar. Could it really be only two days until Juilliard?

He took the turn that led to the Point, but making out was the last thing on his mind. When they got there, he turned off the car and they just stared at each other. Finally Amy spoke.

"I don't want you to go," she whispered.

It probably wasn't physically possible for his

heart to stop, but that's what it felt like—like he simply couldn't go on living with Amy looking at him that way.

"I know," he said. "I don't want to go either. I don't want to leave you."

Amy reached over and ran her hand down his cheek. "These past two weeks have been so . . ."

"Perfect?" Ephram said. "Idyllic? Unbelievably, outrageously incredible?"

She smiled. "I was gonna say weird."

"*'Weird'*?"

"Yeah." Amy leaned in and brushed her lips against his. "After so long being friends, don't you think it's a little weird to do this?" She kissed him again.

"*Good* weird," Ephram murmured. He slipped his arm around her, but she pulled back.

"I mean it, Ephram." Her beautiful eyes were serious. "After Colin, I never thought I'd . . . well, I never expected to feel *normal* again. And I do, with you. I feel healthy. And happy."

"And that's weird?" he asked.

"*Good* weird," she replied, moving in to kiss him again. Ephram held her tight. He felt pretty healthy and happy himself. But it could only last for two more days.

"Concentrate!" Will bellowed.

Ephram barely heard him. Will was always yelling

about focus and concentration—it was his own special way of being a supportive teacher. But how was Ephram supposed to concentrate? The day after tomorrow, he would have to say good-bye to Amy for the rest of the summer. The thought practically made him hyperventilate.

His pinky caught the wrong key and ruined the chord he was on. Ephram figured he would shake it off and keep playing, but Will threw up his hands and stalked out of the room.

Frustrated, Ephram banged the keys. Not too hard—he'd never been so angry that he would disrespect the instrument. He turned on the bench and yelled into the kitchen. "I'm sorry, okay? Forgive me for not being perfect."

"I don't care if you're perfect," Will growled, appearing in the kitchen doorway. "What I care about is dedication. You haven't been practicing."

"Yes, I—"

"No, you haven't, and it shows," Will cut in. Ephram shut up. He *hadn't* been practicing. He'd been going out with Amy. And somehow everything else had ceased to exist. "You're going off to Juilliard in a couple of days and you're rusty. How do you expect to do well there?"

Ephram didn't answer. He had no idea what to say.

"You'll be surrounded by the absolute best players in the country," Will went on. "Folks who spend every waking moment thinking about their music, not their love lives."

Ephram cringed. Will could always tell what was going on with him. He hadn't so much as mentioned Amy's name to his piano teacher, but somehow Will knew that was where his mind was.

"I just started dating the perfect girl," he said.

"Aagh." Will waved him off and disappeared into the kitchen again.

Ephram got up and followed him. "No, I mean it. She's perfect. She's my dream girl." *God, I sound like a dork*, he thought. But what could he do? It was the truth. "And if I go to the Juilliard program, I'll be away from her for almost two months."

"*If* you go?" Will repeated.

Once again, Ephram had no answer. He hadn't even realized what he was saying.

"You told me this was your dream, to go to Juilliard," Will said. "And there's only one way people achieve a dream like that: by dedicating themselves to it, night and day, awake and asleep. Living the music. Living *for* the music."

Ephram nodded. "It *is* my dream," he whispered. It was true. Music was his first love.

"Looks to me like you've got a dream *girl* instead," Will grumbled.

Ephram sat at the kitchen table and dropped his head onto his arms. Piano meant everything to him. Or at least it had until he started going out with Amy. Their relationship was still so new. He couldn't even be sure it would survive a two-month separation. And being with Amy was the thing he wanted most in the world. But did he want it more than he wanted a shot at Juilliard?

"What am I supposed to do?" he asked Will. "I can't choose between Amy and the program."

"Well, you can't shine at Juilliard if you're mooning over some girl," Will said. "You'd better choose."

"What would you do?" Ephram asked.

Will snorted. "I'd get out of here and stop wasting an old man's time," he said, opening the door.

Ephram took the hint and left.

"I'm dying to know what this little breakfast meeting is all about," Amy teased. "I don't usually get phone calls at seven in the morning."

"Yeah, sorry about that. I didn't mean to wake you up." Ephram poured a little milk into Amy's coffee cup. He knew she liked a tiny splash of milk on top of her three heaping spoonfuls of sugar. "But this is important."

Amy picked up her fork and bit into the diner's "special"—French toast made from Wonder Bread. Ephram wrinkled his nose, thinking of a slice of good, thick, New York challah French toast.

"I'm waiting," Amy told him.

"Well . . ." Ephram's palms were sweating. "I'm not going to Juilliard. I'd rather stay here with you," he blurted out. Then he caught his breath, waiting for her to answer. Was she going to freak out? Would she think he was getting too serious too soon?

Amy stared at him for a moment. "You mean you're going to blow off something you really wanted to do because of me? After we've only been going out for two weeks?"

Uh-oh.

"Well, when you put it like that, I sound like a loser," he said.

"No, that's not what I mean. But . . . this summer program was really important to you. I don't want to mess it up." Amy watched him intently.

"You're important to me too," Ephram told her. "And I have an incredible piano teacher right here in Everwood. I'll double up on my lessons with Will. I'll spend all summer practicing every single minute. It will be just as good as going to the program, except I'll still get to see you."

Amy's eyes were shining. "Ephram, you better not be teasing me," she said.

"I'm not." He reached over and took her hand. "So you're happy?"

She bounced on her seat. "Yes! I would've missed you so much!"

Ephram relaxed. She was happy. She didn't think

he was some obsessed stalker. And now he would have a whole summer to be with her.

"But you're sure it's okay?" Amy asked. "I thought this was your last chance to impress those Juilliard guys."

He tried to ignore the little twinge of fear stabbing him in the gut. "Nah, I was being overdramatic. I'm sure I can get in if I just do a kickass audition in the fall." *If they'll even give me another audition after I blow off their program,* he thought.

"Isn't your dad gonna kill you?" Amy asked.

"Yeah." No sense lying about that.

"How are you planning on telling him?"

"I thought I'd get in the car, say it really quick through the window, and then peel out and not go home for a few days."

Amy giggled. "Seriously," she said.

"I don't know." Ephram tried his eggs. They tasted like sawdust. "I think I just have to tell him that it's my decision. He can't force me to go." But the idea of saying that to his father made him feel queasy. He was used to fighting with his dad, but he suspected that this would be much worse—this would be *disappointing* his dad.

"Well, you have to do it today," Amy said gently. "He's expecting to put you on a plane tomorrow."

Ephram nodded.

"You go talk to him," she said. "And then come find me when it's over. We'll spend the whole day together—remind you why you're staying." She squeezed his hand.

Ephram gazed at his beautiful girlfriend—his *girlfriend*!—and smiled. The fight with his father would be bad. And missing the Juilliard program wouldn't be great either. But it was totally worth it as long as Amy would be there, holding his hand and looking at him like that.

It had to be worth it.

Dr. Brown was packing Ephram's piano books into a FedEx box when Ephram got home. Delia sat on the couch watching TV, not even looking up when Ephram walked in. *Maybe I can wait until she's not here,* Ephram thought hopefully, looking for anything possible to put off this conversation with his dad.

"I'm bored," his little sister announced. She clicked off the TV and headed upstairs. *So much for that.*

Ephram turned to his father. "You don't have to do that," he said.

His dad grinned. "It's no problem. I figured I'd ship these out so you don't have to lug them around in your suitcase tomorrow."

Ephram took a deep breath and pictured Amy's face. It was worth it. Staying with Amy was worth missing the program and enduring the impending wrath of Dr. Andy Brown.

"No, I mean you don't have to ship the books." *Because I'm not going,* he silently finished. *I'm not going to Juilliard.*

His father was looking at him suspiciously. "Why not?"

I'm not going, Ephram thought. "I won't need most of those books at the summer program," he said aloud.

"Oh." His dad stopped loading the box.

Ephram's gaze was focused on the thin folder of sheet music in his father's hand. It was Schubert. His mom had given him that piece when he was thirteen.

"What's going on?" Dr. Brown asked.

I'm not going to Juilliard, Ephram thought. "I told Amy I would spend the day with her," he said. "Is that okay?"

"Of course," his father replied. "I'm sure it will be hard to say good-bye."

"Yeah." Ephram slowly sank onto the couch. He was supposed to tell his dad about his decision! Why wouldn't the words come out?

"Listen, Ephram, I know you think I don't approve of Amy," Dr. Brown said. "But that's not the case. I just don't want you to lose sight of what's most important at this point in your life."

"Piano," Ephram murmured, realizing as he said it that his father was right. "Getting into Juilliard. Learning everything I can this summer."

"Exactly!" Dr. Brown began unpacking the box of piano books.

Ephram sat frozen on the couch. How could he have been so stupid? Of course he had to go to New York this summer. It was his only shot at going to school where he wanted, his one chance to build the kind of life he'd always imagined. The kind of life his mom had wanted for him. He couldn't let anyone stand in the way of that. Not even Amy.

"How am I going to tell Amy?" he whispered.

"Tell her what?"

Ephram turned to his father. "She doesn't want me to go," he said. "And I don't want to leave her."

Dr. Brown sat down next to him. "I know you don't. But it's only for the summer."

"We just got together," Ephram said. "How are we supposed to be apart for two months? What if we just . . . fizzle?" He was ashamed of the tears pricking at the back of his eyes. "It's taken so long for us to finally get to this level. . . ."

His father put an arm around his shoulders. "I know, son. I know how much Amy means to you."

"Am I really supposed to choose piano over her?"

"How would you feel if you chose Amy over the piano?" his dad asked.

Happy for half an hour and then miserable, Ephram thought, remembering how right it had felt to tell Amy that he was staying. "I can't," he replied. "I think I love Amy, but I loved music first. And it's my whole life. My whole future."

"I'm sure Amy will understand that," his father said. "You're not choosing *against* her. You're choosing *for* your future."

"But what if she's not waiting for me when I come back?"

Dr. Brown sighed. "I don't know what to tell you, Ephram. Relationships are tricky. Sometimes the long-distance thing is too hard. But I suspect that when that happens, the relationship wasn't meant to be."

Ephram groaned. "That's so not comforting."

"What I mean is that you and Amy have been through a lot together and you're still friends. I have a feeling you'll get through this, too."

Ephram took a shaky breath. His father had been right about Madison. Now all Ephram could do was hope his dad was right about Amy.

Amy knew the second she saw Ephram's face that he was leaving. This morning he'd been all lit up and happy. And now, just a few hours later, he was pale and miserable.

He walked slowly toward her as she waited on the park bench where they had agreed to meet. Amy felt her heart pounding hard in anticipation of what he had to say. She willed herself not to cry.

"Hey." Ephram sat next to her.

"Hey."

"So I talked to my dad," he began.

"He's making you go?" she interrupted. Why hadn't she seen this coming? Of course Dr. Brown wasn't going to just let Ephram blow off the piano program.

"Um, no." Ephram turned to look her in the eye. "I started to tell him I was going to stay here, and then I just . . . didn't."

"Oh." Amy wasn't sure what to say. "Did you, um, did you change your mind about us?"

"No. God, no, Amy." Ephram took her hands and held them tight. "I wish I could be with you every second of every day. But this Juilliard thing . . . it's my only chance. There's no way I'm getting into Juilliard on my own. Going to their summer program will give them the chance to see—"

"It's okay," Amy said quickly. "I understand."

He searched her face. "You do?"

"Yeah." She tried a smile, but it didn't really work. "Piano is so important to you. I know that. It's your whole life."

"No, it isn't. You're important too."

Amy looked into his worried blue eyes. She believed him. She knew Ephram loved her, and that he had loved her all along, ever since they met. If he felt he had to go to Juilliard, then he had to go. She knew him too well to think it had anything to do with wanting to leave her.

"I'm kind of jealous, actually," she told him. "I don't have anything like that in my life—you know, something I totally adore and want to do. It used to be Colin. . . ." Her voice trailed off. She realized how pathetic she sounded, but it was the truth. She'd always been smart and interested in school, but she hadn't been passionate about anything except Colin Hart. Whatever his interests were, she adopted them. She cared about what he cared about. And it wasn't until he died that she realized she didn't have anything of her own—not even one legitimate interest or desire.

Ephram was staring at his sneakers. "I didn't mean to sound like a crybaby," she said. "I just mean that I get it. You want to play piano. You should. You're great at it. Hey, maybe I'll use the summer to figure out what *I* want to do."

"That's what I'm afraid of," Ephram said.

"What do you mean?"

"Maybe you'll figure out that you'd rather find a local boyfriend."

Amy's mouth dropped open. He really could be dense sometimes. "Ephram, no." She leaned over, forcing him to look at her. "I don't want anyone but you. I feel so incredibly lucky that you still want to be with me after everything I put you through. I'm not going anywhere."

Impulsively, she kissed him, willing him to understand how much she cared about him.

He pulled back. "So we're still together?" he asked. "Even when I'm in New York? You'll wait for me?"

"Of course," she promised him. "I'm your girl, don't you know that?"

Ephram looked so relieved that she had to smile. And she did a pretty good job of pretending to be happy for the rest of the afternoon. She didn't want Ephram to go away remembering a sad, mopey girlfriend.

But the minute she got home that night, the tears began to flow. She crumpled onto the couch and let herself cry. Why did it seem like every time things started to go right for her, something came along to ruin it? After Colin's death, and then her depression, and the whole Tommy disaster that followed, she'd figured she was done with sadness for a while. She'd allowed herself to think that maybe she and Ephram could just relax and be happy. But no. Now she was going to be lonely all summer. Their relationship had barely even started, and already it had to be put on hold.

"Care to talk about it?" Her father's voice cut through her quiet sobs.

Amy sat up, surprised. "I thought everyone was in bed," she said, wiping her eyes. "I didn't mean to wake you."

Dr. Abbott shrugged and sat down on the chair

across from her. "I can never sleep after eating your mother's lasagna," he said, rubbing his stomach.

Amy smiled. "I'm glad I missed it."

"So what's wrong?"

"Oh . . ." She leaned back against the soft couch cushions and studied her father's face. He didn't like Ephram. Should she even bother telling him what was wrong? There had been a time when she had told her father everything, but lately things hadn't been so great between them.

"You're not crying in the middle of the night for no reason," her dad said. "It's that Brown creature, isn't it? You had a bad date with him."

"No, Dad, I had a great time with Ephram." Amy sighed. "But he's leaving tomorrow for Juilliard . . . for the rest of the summer."

"Oh. Good."

Amy threw up her hands. "No," she snapped. "It's not good. It sucks. We had finally gotten together and now we have to be thousands of miles away from each other. And it was a stupid roller-coaster day, because he told me he was gonna stay. Then when he decided to go after all, it made the whole thing worse."

At some point she had started crying again. Just thinking about how psyched she'd been this morning made the tears fall even faster. "It isn't fair," she murmured.

"I'm sorry, honey," her dad said. "I know you

like him. But it's only for a few months."

"A few months of sitting around missing him," she replied.

"Funny you should mention that." Her father stood up and began pacing back and forth in front of the couch. That was never a good sign.

"What?" she demanded. "What's going on?"

"Well, I talked to an old friend of mine today, a pal from medical school."

"And?"

"He's in the biochem department at UC Boulder," Dr. Abbott went on.

"Dad, get to the point!" Amy cried. "What does this have to do with me?"

"UC Boulder runs a summer academic program in the sciences," her father said. "I enrolled you in it."

"*What?*" Amy could barely believe her ears. "You put me in summer school?"

"This is an advanced program for gifted high school students," her dad told her. "I'd hardly call it summer school."

"But, Dad, I almost failed chemistry." Amy felt tears returning, but this time they had nothing to do with Ephram. Whenever she thought about how badly she'd done in school this year, she wanted to cry. She knew how much she had let her father down.

"I talked to your principal. He's agreed to put

you in AP physics next year just like you always planned—*if* you do well in this summer class."

"So he'll forget I got a D?"

"You'll be taking an intensive biochemistry class at Boulder. That more than makes up for it. Do well there and your bad grade will be erased."

"But aren't all the other people in the program gonna be really smart?" Amy asked. "I mean, they didn't fail chem, right?"

Dr. Abbott softened. He leaned down and pushed her bangs off her face. "Honey, no one is smarter than you," he said gently. "You've just lost your self-confidence. This summer away will be good for you."

"Away? I'm supposed to live at UC Boulder just for one class?"

"Well, it's pretty intense." Her father stood up. "So you'll be living in the dorms, yes. And believe me, you'll be so busy that I bet you'll never even think about Ephram Brown."

CHAPTER 3

~

"I love New York!" a rage-filled voice shouted. Ephram glanced around, but he couldn't see the ranter. He knew how the guy felt, though. Ephram himself was less than ecstatic that Juilliard's summer program had been moved to Bucks Hollow, Connecticut—*Connecticut!*—due to some flood damage to Juilliard's buildings. He'd been counting on Manhattan to keep him sane while he was away from Amy. There was always some kind of distraction available in the city. But almost as soon as he'd arrived, he'd heard the bad news. And a three-hour bus ride later, he was in Connecticut.

Still, looking around, he knew Bucks Hollow was exactly where his mom would've wanted him to be. It was gorgeous, classy, and refined, just the way she liked things. Stately old brick buildings covered in ivy, cobblestone walkways through the formal gardens, a dormitory that had once been the servants' quarters of this ritzy old estate. Ephram smiled. The servants at Bucks Hollow had lived better than most people he knew!

"Welcome to Juilliard North," joked the thin, gray-haired man waiting in the doorway of the Main Hall. "Name?"

"Ephram Brown," Ephram said.

The man scanned the list he was holding. "Practice room H, second floor. Your placement audition is in one hour. Stay in the room, the faculty will come to you."

It took a few seconds for Ephram to process what he had just heard. "Um, I just got here," he replied, bewildered. He gestured to his two suitcases as if to prove his point.

"Yes," the man said politely.

"I haven't even moved into my room yet," Ephram told him. "I didn't expect to be auditioning today." *I didn't expect to be doing* anything *today,* he thought.

"Yes. The audition is to place you in a performance group," the man said. "There are five groups, from top players to those who need more work. Once you've been placed, you'll be assigned a dormitory room near the others in your performance group."

"Oh." Ephram wasn't sure what else to say.

"Practice room H. That will be your practice room for the rest of the semester."

"Okay. Thanks." Obviously the guy wanted him to move on. Ephram picked up his suitcases and headed into the old building. Bucks Hollow had been a mansion owned by Fitzwilliam Buck, an avid music lover who had conveniently died without any children. In his will, he'd directed that his entire estate should be turned into an institution for musical education. To the people who ran the place, that meant turning it into an elite camp that catered to only one instrument at a time. Summer was piano. Over winter break, the violinists came. In the spring, cellists. The camps were renowned for all the different instruments. Bucks Hollow had good breeding, and the institution had been honored to host the students accepted to the Juilliard program—not to mention the faculty.

None of that comforted Ephram as he lugged his heavy bags up the marble steps to the second floor. The thing about old mansions was that they had no elevators. He hadn't expected to be dragging luggage around with him all day, and he certainly hadn't expected that he would have to play. He was exhausted from the long bus ride. All he wanted to do was take a nap.

But first he had to warm up. He found his practice room at the end of a long hall of identical small, soundproof rooms. Each one contained a student furiously playing piano. Not one of them even glanced up as he walked by. Ephram couldn't hear what they were playing, but it was clear by looking at them that these people were serious.

He left one of his suitcases out in the hallway because it wouldn't fit through the door, and wedged the other one into a corner of the little room. Then he sat down at the piano and placed his fingers on the keys. Nothing came to him. He felt a cold wave of nervousness wash over him. Why hadn't Will told him he'd have to audition right away? He'd sort of been looking forward to getting into his room and calling Amy. It already seemed like ages since he'd seen her. But that wasn't an option.

"Concentrate," he whispered. "This is your only chance."

Miraculously, that seemed to work. He began playing scales to warm himself up. So far Bucks Hollow was a little overwhelming, but he would just have to get over it. He was here for one thing and one thing only: to kick some ass and get himself into Juilliard after he graduated. That was the reason he'd said good-bye to Amy, so piano camp had better be worth it. He finished his scales and moved on to an Art Tatum piece he'd been working on with Will. The jazz calmed him down, and soon he was lost in the music.

When the two teachers arrived for his audition,

Ephram moved effortlessly from the Tatum piece to a Beethoven sonata. He played whatever they wanted without leaving the zone. And when they left, he sat still on his piano bench, eyes closed, remembering the music.

This was what he loved: music—creating it, listening to it, *feeling* it.

Satisfied, he opened his eyes and looked around. The teachers had left the door of his practice room open and there was a petite African-American girl standing in the doorway, staring at him. Ephram jumped in surprise.

"Sorry!" she said, laughing. "I was coming over to say hi but you were meditating or something."

The blood rushed to Ephram's cheeks. He must've looked like an idiot, sitting there with his eyes closed and a goofy grin on his face. "No, I was just . . . decompressing."

"I hear you." The girl perched on top of Ephram's suitcase in the hallway. She was so tiny that her feet didn't even reach the ground when she sat on the bag. "They really throw ya right into things here."

"Yeah." Ephram stuck out his hand. "I'm Ephram Brown."

"Zoe Williams." They shook, her small hand disappearing inside Ephram's grip.

"Don't take this the wrong way," Ephram said. "But how on earth do you reach an octave when your hands are the size of a five-year-old's?"

Zoe giggled, her brown eyes dancing. "Are you telling me you didn't play piano when you were five?"

"No, I did," Ephram said. "But it was harder."

"Well, there's your answer," Zoe told him. "I just work hard at it. Now how about some background?" She smacked the side of the suitcase she was sitting on. "You're not from around here."

"I'm from Colorado," Ephram said. Then he grimaced. "I'm still not used to saying that. I don't *feel* like I'm from Colorado. I've only lived there for two years. I'm originally from New York."

"That explains why you're cool," Zoe said. "You don't seem like a hick from Colorado."

Ephram frowned. Somehow he felt insulted by that, even though it was pretty much what he went around thinking most of the time in Everwood. "They're not *all* hicks," he protested weakly.

"I'll just have to take your word for that," Zoe said. "Couldn't pay me to leave Manhattan. I had a freak fit when I found out the Juilliard program had to be moved out here. But what was I going to do? Best piano professors in the country. Besides, most of the people here are from New York anyway, so it feels like home."

"Cool," Ephram replied. "Do you think they have pizza?"

She grinned. "You miss the real stuff, huh?"

"They should be ashamed to call it pizza in Colorado," he agreed.

Zoe hopped off the suitcase. "The dining room's downstairs across from the concert hall. I'll go with you. I'm starving."

She somehow helped him shove his enormous suitcase into the practice room and close the door. Then she led the way back down the marble staircase and through a maze of halls to the dining room.

Zoe babbled on and on about her piano camp philosophy the entire way to the dining hall. "You've got to get the Juilliard scouts to know you, so they'll remember you when it's time to decide who gets in or not. By this time, I figure they'll think I'm their best friend! And that helps, but I've still got to wow the scouts at the final concert. If you suck, you suck, you know?"

"Great," Ephram muttered. "So I'm basically screwed, since I haven't been making 'best friends' for years?"

Zoe shrugged. "You'll just have to find another way to make yourself memorable." She pushed open the heavy wooden door to the dining room. Inside were about ten big tables covered with food on china plates. But nobody was sitting down. Instead at least thirty people stood crowded around a bulletin board near the kitchen.

Zoe grabbed his arm. "They must've posted the

rankings already. You were one of the last to audition." She charged across the room, dragging Ephram after her. He didn't know why she was bothering to hurry—the crowd around the bulletin board was so thick that they obviously weren't getting anywhere near it for at least five minutes.

"Wait here," Zoe said. She wormed her way in between two other kids and vanished into the mass of bodies. Within a minute she was back.

"I guess sometimes it pays to be small," Ephram said.

"No joke. I can fit places where no one else would dare to go." Zoe grinned up at him. "So do you want the good news or the good news?"

"Both," Ephram told her.

"Good news A: We both placed in the top group," Zoe said happily. "Which means good news B: We're both assigned rooms on the same floor. We're neighbors!"

Amy looked around the dorm room and sighed. Ugly green cinderblock walls, two small beds, two identical desks, two identical dressers.

"It's gonna be a long summer," she muttered.

"Excuse me?" Amy's roommate, Jennifer, asked as she busily set up her textbooks in a neat row on her desk.

"I just mean . . . it's kind of an ugly room," Amy said. "No personality."

Jennifer glanced around, then shrugged. "I guess." She went back to arranging her desk.

Amy picked up the plastic bag full of chemistry books her father had bought her that afternoon. There were three of them, and each one weighed about ten pounds. She dumped them on the desk, then sat down and studied the course syllabus they'd given her when she registered. Classes started tomorrow, and she was supposed to read three chapters before then.

"It's gonna be a long summer," she said again.

"So how's Connecticut?" Amy asked. "Fun so far?" She sounded groggy, and Ephram felt bad for waking her up so early. It wasn't even six A.M. in Colorado. But his schedule had him starting his days at eight o'clock sharp, which meant that the only time he had to call Amy during the day was first thing in the morning. Unfortunately, because of the time difference, Amy would have to wake up at dawn just to talk to him.

"No. It's like boot camp," Ephram complained. "I mean, I knew there'd be a lot of piano. But I figured since we're sort of in the country here at Bucks Hollow there might also be, you know, camp stuff. Swimming and barbeques and nap time."

"I don't think nap time is camp, Ephram. I think it's kindergarten."

"I know. I'm still jet-lagged. All I can think of is sleep. And you."

Amy made a cute little noise that might have been an "awww" or might have been a yawn.

"I can't believe this schedule," he went on. "I'm supposed to work with my teacher for two hours a day and then practice for eight hours a day on top of that. When am I supposed to eat?"

There was a knock on his door. Ephram went to answer it while Amy was talking. "I have a feeling my summer school thing is going to be intense too," she said. "I had six hours of homework yesterday and classes haven't even started yet."

Ephram opened the door to find Zoe waiting in the hallway. She held up a bagel and waved it back and forth under Ephram's nose. "East Coast bagels for the Colorado boy!"

"That *really* smells good," Ephram had to admit.

"What?" Amy asked.

"Oh, nothing. Breakfast," he told her. "I've gotta run and eat or I'll have to go hungry until after my two-hour-long class."

"Okay. Good luck," Amy said.

"You too. Let me know how the first day goes."

Zoe was setting up a little feast of bagels and cream cheese on his desk. "Who was that?" she asked.

"Uh, my girlfriend." Ephram had to force his mouth into a normal position—he still wanted to grin like a fool whenever he called Amy that.

"From Colorado?" Zoe asked, taking a bite of bagel.

"Yup."

"Sweet," she replied dismissively. "So you're meeting Ms. Kinney today!"

Ephram was a little surprised at the topic change, but he went with it. "Yeah. Do you know her?"

"I had her last year. She's good. She really knows what the scouts like."

"Can she play?"

Zoe rolled her eyes. "Who cares? As long as she can help you get in, she's good in my book. Eat up. We're gonna be late."

It's a good thing Zoe's here to boss me around, Ephram thought wryly as he entered his practice room. If she hadn't come by, he definitely would have been late, and he had a feeling Ms. Kinney wouldn't have let him get away with that. She was sitting on the one chair squeezed into the corner of the practice room, and she was not smiling.

"Hi, I'm Ephram Brown," he said. "You must be Ms. Kinney?"

"Yes. Sit down, start with scales."

Okay, not too much with the small talk, he thought. That was all right. Will wasn't much of a chatter, either. But Will was large and round and sort of teddy bearish, even though he didn't want to be. Ms. Kinney was thin and bony and angular.

Ephram got the feeling he could cut himself on her if he wasn't careful.

"I've been working with Will Cleveland out in Everwood," he said. "Do you know him?"

"No, and I'd like to concentrate on your technique." She shot him an exasperated look. "No talking, please. I'm listening to you play."

"Sorry," he mumbled. This summer was going to be no fun at all.

After Ephram warmed up, Ms. Kinney pulled out five pieces of music and lined them up on the stand. "We'll focus on these for the summer. In a week or two we'll narrow it down to one, which you'll play for your midpoint recital and also for your final recital."

Ephram scanned the music—Bach, Beethoven, Haydn, Mendelssohn, and Mozart. "These seem sort of . . . standard," he said.

Ms. Kinney raised one thin eyebrow. "Meaning?"

"Well, they seem boring," Ephram admitted. "I've played them all before. *Everyone* has played them all before."

"It's not the amount of times you've played it that matters to us at Juilliard," she said. "It's how well you play."

"I know, but . . . I've been playing mostly jazz with my teacher at home. Couldn't I play something by Art Tatum? Or Oscar Peterson?"

Ms. Kinney laughed for the first time. "Absolutely

not," she snorted. "I'm off to meet my next student. We'll start regular classes tomorrow. Today, I want you to spend the two hours practicing. I suggest you start with the Bach."

The second the door closed behind her, leaving him alone in his soundproof cocoon, Ephram started on the Art Tatum piece Will had given him.

Amy dropped her head onto her book. She'd been studying for hours, after sitting in class all day long. Was this really what college was going to be like?

She needed a study break. Grabbing her cell, she hit the speed dial for Ephram's number. But it went straight to his voice mail. He never brought his phone into the practice room with him—it was against the rules. Amy sighed, frustrated. They only got to speak to each other early in the morning or late at night, and one of them was always too tired to talk for long. Even though she spoke to Ephram every day, she missed him. A lot.

Amy turned back to her book. Her eyes were practically crossing from reading such small type. She glanced over at Jennifer, who was studying as usual, scribbling notes in the margins of her book.

"I need a study break," Amy said. "You want to go grab a cup of coffee?"

Jennifer jumped as if Amy had just shot off the starting pistol at a race.

"Oh. Wow. Sorry," Amy said. "Didn't mean to scare you."

"I was concentrating," Jennifer said accusingly.

"Yeah, I can see that." Amy forced a smile. "Well, since I already interrupted you, do you want to take a break? Get some coffee?"

"I don't drink coffee."

"Okay. We can do something else," Amy said. "There's an ice-cream place right—"

"No, thank you," Jennifer cut in. "We have a lot of work to do. There's no time for ice cream."

Amy bit her lip. "I just can't study for so long without a rest."

"Maybe you should take a walk or something," Jennifer said pointedly.

"Yeah, good idea." Amy grabbed her room key and left without saying good-bye. She'd never met such an automaton before. Why did she have to get stuck with the roommate who had no personality?

At the end of the bland hallway was an equally bland little student lounge, where there were two cheap couches and an ancient TV. Amy headed for the lounge, hoping that a little television would clear her mind. She'd watch something for an hour or so, then Ephram would be done with practice so she could call him. Maybe she could fit in a little more studying before bed.

The lounge was almost full. Three out of the

four places on the couches were taken up by students reading. It was dead silent.

"Um, I was gonna watch some TV," Amy said.

No one answered. "Okay then," she muttered. If they weren't even going to be polite enough to acknowledge her, she'd just ignore them, too. She went over to the TV and clicked it on.

"Hey!" cried one of the guys. "Turn it off!"

"I just said I was going to turn it *on*," Amy pointed out.

"We're studying," the girl sitting next to him said.

"Can't you study in your room?" Amy asked.

"No," the girl said. "I'm more productive out here."

"Me too," the second guy chimed in.

"I get claustrophobic in my room," the girl added.

"Really? I just fall asleep," the first guy said, turning to phobia girl.

I'm in hell, Amy thought. *I'm surrounded by nerds.*

"This is the lounge," she said, interrupting their conversation. "It's for lounging, not studying. I want to watch TV."

"There are more of us," the girl pointed out. "Majority rules."

"You can study in your rooms or in the library," Amy said. "This is the only place where I can watch television."

The first guy shrugged. "Sorry."

All three of them went back to their books. Amy stared at them, appalled.

She had two options: She could turn the TV up and try to bully them into leaving, or she could give up and go back to her room.

She gave up.

By the time Friday rolled around, Ephram was so tired and sore he could hardly move. His neck hurt. His shoulders hurt. His arms, his hands—even his butt was in pain. He'd never spent so much time sitting at a piano in his life. He had always figured that the upside of being a music geek was that he was safe from muscle aches.

After practice, he collapsed onto the bed in his room and closed his eyes. Amy would still be in the lab. He would sleep for a couple of hours and then call her.

A knock on his door woke him up less than ten minutes later. Ephram groaned. "Go away," he called.

"No," Zoe yelled back from outside in the hall.

Ephram shook his head. She was cool, and she was funny. But she was also like the Energizer Bunny—so high-energy that Ephram couldn't keep up with her. Whenever they had a break in practice, Zoe was there to drag him off to lunch, or for a walk. She never seemed to stop moving.

Ephram rolled off the bed, his back aching in protest. He unlocked the door, then threw himself back down onto the mattress. Zoe pushed open the door and laughed. "What are you, eighty?" she said. "Get changed. There's a party in the lounge."

Ephram groaned again. "What party?"

"Greg from Dalton—you know him, right?"

"Mmph." Ephram did know Greg—they'd been on the same concert circuit when Ephram lived in Manhattan. Back then, Greg had sucked at piano. Ephram had never paid much attention to him.

"He convinced the headmaster to let us use the lounge for a welcome party. You know, kind of a Bucks Hollow–Juilliard mixer—with no chaperones."

"Is he any good now?" Ephram asked. "He was, like, the worst piano player I ever heard."

"No, he's still bad. His dad pays off Bucks Hollow to let him in every year."

Ephram let his head drop back down onto the pillow.

"But he throws good parties." Zoe opened Ephram's closet and began flipping through his shirts. "You've gone native, wardrobe-wise," she commented. "Where are all your black clothes?"

He smiled. In New York his entire wardrobe had been black. But it was nearly impossible to find black *anything* in Everwood. "Doesn't matter. I'm not going to the party," he mumbled.

"Oh, come on. Everyone's going," Zoe said.

"Not me. Couldn't care less about Greg from Dalton." Ephram was half asleep already.

"So what? Come and hang out with *me*," Zoe said. She put her knee on his bed and bounced up and down.

"Ow," Ephram said. "Stop that."

"Just come for an hour," Zoe pressed on.

Ephram sat up and looked her in the eye. "No," he told her. "I have to call Amy."

Zoe rolled her eyes. "Right," she said. "Fine. Be a hermit. See you tomorrow." She breezed out of the room, and Ephram went right back to sleep.

Amy stared at the aluminum foil. She had torn it into a bunch of tiny pieces, and now she had to weigh it in a beaker. Easy. But she still felt the need to check and recheck her measurements at least five times. Finally she had to admit that she knew how much the foil weighed. Now it had to be torn into smaller pieces. She did that. That was easy. And the pieces went into an Erlenmeyer flask. Okay.

She couldn't believe her hands were shaking as she worked. She was on step two of the lab. It was basically still the "gathering materials" phase. But she was totally paranoid that she would do something wrong. At the two other labs this week, her partner, Billy, had done most of the work. But Billy had gone to the infirmary with an asthma attack this morning, so she was on her own.

"Thank god it's Friday, huh?" said a voice in her ear.

Amy tore her eyes away from the foil to see a tall, good-looking guy settling himself on the stool next to her. "Do you mind?" he asked. "I've been working solo all week, but since your partner's gone, I thought I'd sub in."

"Oh. No, that's fine," Amy said. "Why don't you have a partner?"

He shrugged. "An odd number of people. Plus, you don't really *need* partners. These labs are all pretty basic."

As he spoke, he reached for a beaker. "Twenty milliliters of 3 M KOH, coming up," he said. "Excuse me while I take this to the fume hood."

Amy gaped at him.

"Because the hydrogen gas is flammable," he said.

"Right," she said. "Yeah, I know." *Hydrogen gas?* She flipped back through her lab notes as he added the solution to the aluminum foil under the fume hood. Was there supposed to be hydrogen gas?

He was looking at her quizzically. "I'm a little rusty on lab work, to tell you the truth," Amy said. "I kind of skipped a lot of classes this year."

He grinned. "As long as you're smart enough, you can always make up for it, right?"

"That's what I'm hoping," Amy said. "Taking this summer class is supposed to make up for it."

"Cool." He came back to the table and held out

the flask. "You wanna look? It did just what it was supposed to do. Shocker."

Amy laughed. "You're not like all the other people here," she told him. "So far you're the only one who doesn't take this course totally seriously."

"Nah, I'm serious about it," he said. "I'm planning to be premed in college, so I need to do well. But the beginning of class is always easy. When it gets harder later in the semester, then I'll pay more attention."

Amy nodded. "That's how I've always felt about school."

"We're two of a kind." He held out his hand. "I'm Joel Finkel."

"Amy Abbott." She shook his hand, and he held onto hers for a second.

"Truly a pleasure," he said.

"What a line," she commented, pulling her hand back.

Joel chuckled. "It's true. That *was* a line. I'm hoping you'll go out with me. You're the only normal girl here."

"I'm so flattered." Amy's voice was sarcastic, but her heart felt lighter for the first time in days. So far, Joel was the only person here that she could even have a conversation with. "I have a boyfriend," she informed him.

"Of course you do," he said, undeterred. "The pretty ones always do."

"But you'll still be my lab partner, right?" Amy asked. "'Cause you're the only normal *guy* here."

"Sure," Joel said. "And once you get used to me, you'll forget all about that boyfriend."

Amy smiled at him. "Not likely." And it was true. Nothing could make her forget about Ephram—no amount of boring school and no nice lab partner.

But it was good to have a new friend.

"I have to see you," Ephram said. It was midnight on Friday, and he could hear the party raging downstairs. He covered his free ear with his hand so he could hear Amy's voice better on his cell phone.

"How are we gonna do that, Ephram?" she asked.

"I don't know. I don't care," he said. "It's been less than a week and already I'm dying. I miss you."

"I miss you, too."

"So come to Connecticut," Ephram begged. "Come for a weekend."

Amy was silent for a moment. "I *do* have a long weekend over the Fourth of July," she said. "It's right after the midterm exam. I guess they figure we need time to recover."

"So do it," Ephram replied. "Come then. We can go to New York."

"That would be so amazing, Ephram," she said.

"It's the greatest place in the world!" Ephram cajoled.

"I can't afford it," Amy said.

"Can't your parents pay for you? You said you had a break, right?"

"Yeah, but my dad thinks I'm going to go home and spend it with them."

Ephram considered their options. She was right—the Abbotts would want Amy to spend her free time with them. "My father is coming to visit in two weeks," he finally said. "He's bringing Delia."

"Cool."

"Not really. I'm kinda dreading it," Ephram admitted. "I'm so busy. . . ."

"But that's a great idea," Amy said, excitement creeping into her voice. "I'll get my parents to come visit me *here,* and then they'll have to let me go away over the long weekend, because I'll already have spent time with them."

"I doubt your dad will be happy about you visiting me," Ephram said.

"That's why I'll ask my mom," Amy replied. "So let's make it definite. I'll come see you over the Fourth of July. Somehow I'll make it happen."

Ephram's heart beat faster just thinking about Amy. Imagining her in Connecticut, in his room. "I can't wait," he murmured.

Someone turned the music up downstairs. Ephram put his pillow over his head, wrapping himself in a little world where nothing existed but him and Amy. "What else is going on?" he asked.

"Did you find any non-dweebs there yet?"

Amy paused for a moment. "No," she finally said. "I've pretty much given up on that. How about you? Make any new friends?"

Ephram thought about Zoe. She'd been his constant companion all week. But should he tell Amy that?

"No," he said. "No one."

CHAPTER 4

"Your father? That blows," Zoe said.

Ephram nodded. He had gotten used to her bluntness over the past few weeks. "Yeah. It's the last thing I need on top of everything else."

"You still having a pissing contest with Kinney?" Zoe took a big bite of her sandwich.

"I wouldn't call it that, but yes," Ephram said. "I hate the stuff she's got me playing. I'm bored. I want to play jazz."

Zoe frowned. "Look, it's not like I'm in love with Ms. Kinney or anything, but she does know what she's talking about. She teaches at Juilliard, after all. The Juilliard admission scouts will want to hear classical."

Ephram ran his hand through his hair. "Are you sure? Because if I were them, I'd be sick of hearing the same pieces over and over. I might be happy to hear a little jazz for a change."

Zoe narrowed her dark eyes and stared off into space. Ephram knew that look—it was the expression she got when she was plotting something. "That might be it for you," she said slowly.

"What?"

"Well, you're kinda off-track," she said simply. "You haven't been doing New York concerts for a couple of years now. You're out in the boonies without a top-notch teacher. You need to do something attention-worthy. Boldness. It could be what gets you noticed."

Ephram was offended on behalf of himself, of Everwood, and of Will. But he had to admit, Zoe had a point. "And you think playing some Art Tatum at the final recital might be what I need to get the Juilliard scouts to pay attention?"

Zoe nodded. "Could be."

"Huh." The truth was, Ephram didn't care so much what the Juilliard scouts thought. When he had first arrived at Bucks Hollow, he'd thought it was all that mattered. But now, after weeks of being forced to play things he had no passion for, he was beginning to think that maybe there were more important things than Juilliard. Like being true to himself. But maybe he could use Zoe's argument to convince Ms. Kinney to let him play Art Tatum for his recital. It was worth a try.

"Anyway, I don't know what to do with my dad," he said. "The midpoint recital is next week. I don't have time to be baby-sitting him and my sister. I need to practice."

Zoe shrugged. "So send them off sightseeing. There's a historical village about twenty miles from here. That's good for a day. Then there's an ice-cream factory nearby. Your sister should like that."

"You think I can get away with that?" Ephram asked. "It's not rude to make them hang out alone when they're here to visit *me*?"

"I don't know," she said. "Maybe it's rude. Do you care?"

Ephram thought about that. Did he care? A little. His father had his faults, but things had been getting better between them over the past couple of years. He didn't want to hurt the guy's feelings. Still, he had a ton of practicing to do for the recital. He glanced up at Zoe. She wouldn't let a little rudeness interrupt her work on the piano. And the truth was that she reminded him a bit of himself—the way he used to be when he lived in New York. *That* Ephram wouldn't have given a single thought to his father's feelings.

Maybe it was time to let the old Ephram back out for a while.

"So this is the big time, huh?" Dr. Brown boomed. "Nice place."

Ephram cringed. His father's voice was echoing off the marble walls and high ceilings of the Bucks Hollow mansion. Why did he always have to be so loud?

"It's boring," Delia commented. "Can't we go back to the hotel and go swimming?"

Ephram grinned and pushed her baseball cap down over her eyes. His little sister was happiest when she was doing something active. She was the complete opposite of him.

"No, we can't go swimming," his father went on, voice as loud as ever. "We're here to see Ephram, not to hang out in a hotel."

One of the Bucks Hollow teachers stuck her head out of a practice room and frowned at them.

"Sorry," Ephram said. He grabbed his dad's arm and turned him toward the exit. "You know you're loud if they can hear you in a soundproof practice room," he said.

"Oh. Sorry." Dr. Brown didn't sound sorry at all. "So what's next on the tour?"

"You've seen pretty much my whole life," Ephram said. "The practice room and the concert stage. That's all I do."

"Where do you live?" Delia asked.

"Yeah, let's see your room," Dr. Brown agreed.

"Okay." Ephram led them outside and down the cobblestone path to the students' house. "I'm on the top floor," he said, looking up at the highest row of windows. "The whole first level class is on the same floor. I guess they want us to only associate with our own kind."

"Makes sense," his father said, totally missing Ephram's sarcasm.

As he unlocked the door to his room, Zoe stuck her head out of her own room three doors down. "Hey, Ephram," she called. She wandered over and grinned at Delia. "Hey, little sister," she added.

Delia didn't answer. But she did shoot Ephram a pretty scary look of death. Delia liked Amy. Therefore she was *not* going to like any other girl who hung around Ephram. He understood. "Uh, her name's Delia," he told Zoe.

"And I'm Andy Brown," his father put in. "You must be that Joey that Ephram's always talking about."

"Zoe," she corrected him.

"Oh, sorry," Dr. Brown said, still not sounding sorry. "You a budding concert pianist too?"

"Yeah," Zoe told him. "We all are here."

"Really?" He turned to Ephram. "It's all piano? No other instruments?"

"Um, yeah, Dad," Ephram said. "I told you that about twenty times."

"Huh," his father replied. "So, Zoe, maybe you'd like to join us for dinner tonight? Get away from the school food for one evening?"

Delia made a small noise of protest, and Ephram had to hold himself back from doing the same. Just because he hung out with Zoe didn't mean he wanted to involve her in his family life. He had to act fast. "Actually, I can't do dinner tonight," he said quickly. "I mean, neither of us can."

"It's true. I have to practice," Zoe said. "I'm on my way over to the practice rooms now. You coming, Ephram?"

"Yeah," he said. "I'll be there in a minute."

Zoe gave them a little wave and disappeared down the hall. Ephram turned to his dad, who looked stricken. "What do you mean, you can't do dinner?" he asked.

"I just can't," Ephram said. "I'm scheduled for practice time until eight o'clock tonight."

"Well, can't you skip it for one day?" Dr. Brown asked. "Your family is here."

"No, I can't skip it," Ephram said, his voice rising to match his dad's. "I have the mid-point recital next week. I need every minute of practice I can get."

"But you're already good," Delia said.

Ephram looked down at her and sighed. "Thanks," he said. "But I'm not good enough. Why don't you guys go to the historical village today while I'm busy?"

They both stared at him, utterly betrayed.

"Or the ice-cream factory?" he tried.

Delia's face lit up instantly. "Cool!" she cried. Smiling, Ephram glanced at his father, who still looked hurt.

"Okay," Ephram said. "Have fun. I'll see you tomorrow." Then he turned and fled.

When Ephram closed the door of the practice room behind him it was after nine at night. He was exhausted, and the Bach piece sounded the same as it always did. All he wanted to do was go back to his room and call Amy.

But when he got outside into the warm night air, he discovered that his father was waiting for him, sitting on the steps of the mansion.

Ephram felt every muscle in his body clench up. There was only one reason his dad would be there so late at night: a fight. Ephram had seen flies with more control over their anger than the famous Dr. Andy Brown. He decided to go on the offensive. Sometimes he could get his dad to back off that way.

"Where's Delia?" he demanded. "It's late."

"She's in the hotel watching pay-per-view," his father replied, turning at the sound of Ephram's voice. "And hello to you, too."

"Fine," Ephram said. "Hello. Don't you think it's a little dangerous to leave Delia all by herself in a strange place?"

"She has my cell number, and yours," his dad

said. "And she stays home alone for longer than this. And I asked the concierge to keep an eye on the room. And why am I justifying any of this to you?"

So much for that strategy, Ephram thought. "I have to get some sleep," he said. "Did you want something?"

His father stood up, his face red. "Did I *want* something?" he repeated, loud voice growing even louder. "Yes, in fact, I did. I wanted to see my son. Rumor has it he attends this place."

"What's that supposed to mean?"

"It means that when your sister and I fly all the way out here to see you, it would be nice if you made some time for us," his father yelled.

"Would you keep your voice down?" Ephram snapped. "People are trying to sleep."

"Come off it, Ephram. It's not even nine-thirty," his father replied. "I remember being a teenager. I know everyone is probably up partying until two A.M. every night."

"That's it!" Ephram exploded. He was the one yelling now, but he didn't care who overheard. "Partying? You think there's partying going on here? Are you blind? Look around—there are no lights on. There's no music. There's no fun, no happiness, no relaxation. There's nothing but practice."

Ephram noticed a few lights going on—he'd

woken people up. But there was no stopping himself now. All the frustration that had been building up inside him since he got here came pouring out.

"We go to bed at nine o'clock because we have to get up at the crack of dawn to practice," he went on. "Then we practice all day. And at night? We *practice*."

"Ephram—"

"Did you think I was lying?" Ephram cried. "Did you think I just decided to blow you and Delia off because I wanted to?"

"No, of course not—"

"I just couldn't stand the stress of taking time off and trying to act all normal around you when all I would be thinking about was the fact that everyone else was practicing! That they'd be getting ahead of me. And they're already ahead of me—every single person here has a better shot at Juilliard than I do."

His father stared at him, openmouthed. Even Ephram was surprised by his outburst. He hadn't realized how much this workload was getting to him.

"You told me you placed in the top-level class," Dr. Brown said.

"I did," Ephram muttered. "So what? The other people in my level have already played a million concerts for the Juilliard scouts. They live in New York. The scouts know them. But I have one chance, just this one stupid final concert. And it has to be good enough that they remember me when it comes time to decide who gets in. Good enough that I stand out from all these other people they've been watching for years—" His voice broke and he sat down on the marble steps.

"Good enough to make up for all the time you lost after your mother died," his father finished. Dr. Brown sat down next to him. All his anger was gone. "I'm sorry, Ephram," he said. "I didn't think to get you a piano tutor when we moved to Colorado. I was so overwhelmed by everything. . . ."

"It doesn't matter," Ephram said. "I couldn't have played then anyway."

They sat for a moment in silence.

"Maybe this was too much," his father finally said. "This program . . . I knew it was intensive, but I didn't realize *how* intensive. Maybe you just aren't ready for this level of work yet."

Ephram stared down at his sneakers. If he wasn't ready for the Juilliard summer program, then he certainly wasn't ready for Juilliard. He wasn't ready for his future. "I can't accept that," he said quietly.

"There's no shame in it," his dad said, looking him in the eye. "You're stressed out. This isn't what you love about piano."

"I wouldn't be so stressed if I could just do what I love," Ephram blurted out. "But they won't let me." He realized that he sounded like a whiny five-year-old. And part of him hoped his father would somehow make it all better, the way fathers were supposed to.

"What do you mean?"

"My teacher says I have to play Bach at my recital," Ephram explained. "I'm sick of Bach. And Beethoven. I'm sick of classical."

"You're playing jazz with Will," Dr. Brown said.

"Exactly!" Ephram exclaimed, excitement building inside him. Just thinking about playing jazz, instead of the stuffy, old pieces he was working on, made him loosen up. "That's what I want to do. That's what I dream about at night. I play Bach all day and then I dream of Art Tatum."

His father studied Ephram's face, which was flushed with enthusiasm. "That's more like it," he said. "Why won't they let you play jazz?"

"Ms. Kinney says the Juilliard scouts won't like it."

"Do you believe her?"

Ephram shrugged. "Kinney's a Juilliard professor. She's part of their program. And even the Bucks Hollow people who aren't with Juilliard get a lot of their students into the school. They must know what they're talking about."

"Okay then." His dad clapped him on the shoulder as if they'd reached some sort of decision.

"Okay what?" Ephram asked.

"You have a clear choice," Dr. Brown said. "Either you play what you love, or you play what Juilliard wants. But ask yourself this, Ephram: If Juilliard won't let you do what you love, do you really think it's the right place for you?"

Ephram had been practicing for an hour before Ms. Kinney showed up the next day. She gave him a cursory smile. "Ready to get started?" she asked.

Ephram cleared his throat. "Yes. On the piece *I've* chosen."

Ms. Kinney glanced at him in surprise. "I thought we'd agreed on the Bach," she said. "Did you want to reconsider Mozart?"

"No, I want *you* to reconsider jazz," Ephram said. "I have a piece by Art Tatum. It's amazing— complicated, emotional . . ."

She was shaking her head.

"Why not?" he asked. To his astonishment, he sounded just like his father: belligerent.

Ms. Kinney pursed her thin lips together. "Because it simply isn't done, Ephram."

"Well, I'm doing it," he announced.

"Even if it loses you a shot at Juilliard?"

"Yes," Ephram said, sure of himself for the first time since he got to Bucks Hollow. "If I can't play jazz for Juilliard, then it's not where I want to be."

CHAPTER 5

"Wait, you're putting that dot in the wrong place. We haven't tried that wavelength on the sample yet," Amy protested.

"Have you looked outside?" Joel asked, adding more dots to the graph—dots that shouldn't be there because they hadn't done the part of the experiment that would give them the data.

"Let's see. Chemistry lecture all morning. Forty-five minutes for lunch, thirty of which were spent filling in gaps in my notes left by the extreme fast-talking of Dr. Semel, who clearly aspires to be an auctioneer. Then chemistry lab," Amy rattled off. "So no. I have not looked outside."

"That's what I thought." Joel lowered his voice. "And since you and I both know exactly how this *experiment* is going to turn out . . ."

"We do?"

"Yeah. The Chromium (III) absorption spectrum is shown in pretty much every textbook." He connected the dots on the graph, forming a curve. "I say we turn in our lab notebook and go out and play."

Amy glanced around the lab. Gray work tables, shades drawn, heads bent over tungsten lamps and graphs. Suddenly it felt like there was no oxygen in the room. And she had seen the absorption spectrum before. . . . At least, she was pretty sure she had. It wouldn't hurt to escape for a few hours.

Joel gave her a naughty-boy grin. "Where do you think Ms. Fuller really took off to? Do you really believe she had to leave early to get a filling replaced? She just couldn't stand another second in here." He grabbed Amy's backpack off the floor and held it out to her.

Just a couple of hours, she promised herself as she closed her hand around the strap of the backpack. She needed the time to fortify herself for her parents' visit. It wasn't that she didn't want to see them. It was more that she didn't want them to see *her*. Being away from the constant scrutiny of her parents was the only good thing about Boulder so far.

"Come on," Joel whispered. He had already stashed the lamp. They tiptoed to the front of the room, put their lab book in Ms. Fuller's in-box, and slipped into the hallway. Without saying a word, they began to walk faster and faster. By the time they reached the main doors and burst into the quad, they were running.

"Freedom!" Joel yelled.

Amy tilted her head back and closed her eyes, letting the sun hit her face full-force. It was actually summer. Cooped up in classes all day, she had forgotten what that meant.

"I'm thinkin' City Park. We can rent skates. Unless you brought some?"

"My dad kind of supervised my packing," Amy admitted. Then she wished she had kept her mouth shut. Why not just stick a name tag on her chest: *Hi, I'm Amy, former juvenile delinquent.* "Um, he doesn't believe in studying on skates."

"It *can* make you dizzy. But I'm pre-premed. I'll be able to handle any skating mishaps." He grinned again. She was starting to think of it as the Grin. It was too big not to have a name of its own.

Thirty-five minutes later, she, Joel, and the Grin were zinging around Denver's biggest park—complete with zoo, IMAX theater, band shell, lake, golf course, and natural history museum. Amy tried to remember the last time she was on skates. Not with Tommy, that's for sure. She wondered if Ephram had *ever* been on skates. Trying to picture it made her smile. Not that he was a klutz. He was just more of an indoor kind of guy.

"Ahh, my skyting therapeez, she is verking." Joel's Dr. Freud accent sucked. It sucked so bad it made her giggle. And suddenly it was like the air she was breathing was replaced with helium. Everything seemed funny. Tourists in the paddle boats: funny. Brown-and-black mutt almost tripping Joel: funny. Artist trying to sell bad portraits: very funny. A mom, a dad, and a teenage boy, licking ice-cream cones and clearly having absolutely nothing to say to each other . . .

Not so funny.

The sun was still warm. The breeze created by the speed of Amy's skating was still blowing her hair away from her face. It still felt good to be moving her muscles. The park was still beautiful. There was still great people-watching to be had. But Amy couldn't take pleasure in any of it anymore. Her giggles were over.

Joel grabbed her hand and pulled her over to the nearest unoccupied patch of grass. "I need a break." He flopped onto his back.

Amy unlaced her skates, pulled them off, and then decided to ditch her socks, too, so she could feel the grass between her toes. Nothing said summer more than bare feet meeting grass. But it was no use. That summertime feeling was gone.

"You can use this time to tell me all about it." Joel turned his head toward Amy, shading his eyes with his arm.

"About what?" Amy bluffed.

"About why I was skating along with a happy girl, then suddenly I'm with a zombie."

Amy rolled her eyes. He'd gone exactly where she hadn't wanted him to go. "Zombie is a little hyperbolic."

"I guess. I mean, I didn't see any flesh-eating."

Good, he's going to drop it, Amy thought.

"But you do seem kinda stressed or something all of a sudden. I thought you might want to—"

"Tell you all about it so you can fix it for me? Are you one of those kinds of guys? I hate them," Amy snapped. Her father was like that. He'd just decided that taking this stupid chem class so she could still take AP classes next year was exactly what she needed, and *wham,* strings were pulled, and here she was. No "Amy, do you want to be in AP?" or anything resembling that.

"Hell, no. I hate those guys too. Always shoving in where they're not wanted, trying to be nice." The Grin appeared.

Amy smiled back. She couldn't help herself. Obviously Joel wasn't anything like her father. She would do the same thing if she noticed that something was bothering him. She'd ask him what was wrong. Maybe she wouldn't try to fix it, but she'd listen. And maybe a little venting was exactly what she needed.

"Okay," she said. "My parents are coming to visit tomorrow."

Joel sat up. "Your parents? Here? I can help you move your stuff out tonight!"

Amy grabbed a handful of grass and threw it at him, the way she would at Bright. "Shut up. It's just that I know it's going to feel more like an inspection . . . or a psychiatric evaluation."

"That strict, huh?" Joel flicked a blade of grass off his nose.

Amy decided to go for the truth. Why not? Everyone in Everwood knew. What did it matter if one more person did? "They had some help. I got involved with a guy who was . . ." She hesitated. It was so hard to describe Tommy, even now. Vulnerable? Damaged? Needy? A liar? An addict? "He was a drug dealer, and he was using," she continued. "And I guess I was trying to be one of those fix-it people I claim to hate so much. I thought I could save him. I wanted to be that person, that person who was so important."

She pulled up another handful of grass, clumps of dirt coming with it. She stared at the empty patch she'd made in the smooth green carpet. She hadn't meant to do that.

Amy glanced at Joel. He was simply waiting, giving her as much time as she needed. "And while I was trying to do that, I . . . let's see, I stopped caring about school and failed some classes—this from an A student—I basically broke my parents' hearts, ruined my brother's senior year, threw away a guy I really loved, and, oh yeah, got really, really drunk and took some GHB."

Joel didn't answer for a long moment. Amy was glad he didn't. At least he was thinking about what she'd said. He wasn't going to just spew some variation of "It's not that bad," while clearly wishing he had never asked.

"I guess you're probably right about the inspection-slash-evaluation. It'll probably be like that for a while with your parents. What you described . . . not easy to forget." Joel retied the laces on one of his skates while he continued to talk. "But you're pulling it together. You're here, right? And more important, your parents let you come. To a big city. By yourself. So that means there's some trust, right?"

Amy nodded. She hadn't really thought of it that way, but her parents were letting her live in Boulder alone and unsupervised. "I really do want to see them," she told Joel. *I just wish somehow I could do it without them seeing* me, she silently added.

Sadly, she was completely visible when her parents showed up at her dorm room at eight o'clock the next morning. Amy made a big deal of introducing them to Jennifer, who was already up and studying. Jennifer was definitely the kind of thing that Amy wanted her parents to see today. And with Jennifer in the room, there were no questions asked that Amy didn't want to answer. Even the probing looks were kept to a minimum.

That changed the second Amy and her parents stepped into the hall. "What do you want to see first?" Amy asked—at the exact same moment that her father began questioning her about the curriculum and her mother commented on her complexion.

It wasn't the first time they'd all started talking at once. But this time, instead of laughter followed by a round of "I'll go," "No, let me go first," there was an awkward silence. Glances flew from face to face as they all tried to assess who was going to speak. Politeness. That's what it was. And until now, that had never been part of the Abbott family culture.

For Amy it was like a slap in the face. This was what she'd done to her family: made them stiff and unnatural with each other. "Um, I did get a little sun, Mom. I went skating," Amy said, thinking that her mother would be pleased she'd gotten some outdoor exercise. "And, Dad, in lab we just did an absorption spectra experiment." *Please don't ask about it,* she thought. She hadn't had a chance to sit down and really figure out what should have happened if they'd actually done the whole experiment yesterday, although she was definitely planning to. "If you want, I can go back and get my textbook and lecture notes. It'll be easier to go over the classwork that way."

"We can do that later," her father said. "I'm interested in meeting your professor. You said he taught at the college during the regular term."

Amy nodded. This was good; her dad would enjoy this. "Right. Dr. Semel. He covers a ton in every lecture." *Because he talks so unbelievably fast*, she added to herself.

"Do you know where he got his degree?" her father asked.

"Could we have this conversation somewhere else?" her mom said. "On the way to the cafeteria, perhaps? Don't you want some breakfast, Amy?"

Amy really didn't. Her stomach felt like it was sitting in a pan in one of the bio labs, being poked and prodded. But if she didn't want to eat, her mother would worry. And for Amy, this visit was all about reassurance. "Breakfast, sure. The cafeteria is this way." She started down the hall. "Um, I don't know where Dr. Semel got his degree, Dad. But if we spot a catalog along the way, we can look in the back. It'll probably say in his biography."

The short walk from the dorm to the cafeteria was fine. Nice, chit-chatty, polite. Not at all like how her family usually acted. But Amy figured that if they had to be polite for a while in order to make things better, she could handle it. Eventually everything would go back to normal. Maybe it was like coming up from a deep sea dive. If you did it too fast, you could die, right?

"You can get all kinds of stuff with your food card," Amy explained as she led the way inside. "There's always eggs and all kinds of hot stuff at breakfast, and a salad bar at lunch and dinner, plus a bunch of choices. And you can also get yogurt and fruit. Or sandwiches and burritos and burgers every day."

She grabbed an OJ, then thinking of her mother, added an order of scrambled eggs to her tray. The place was pretty deserted. Even most of the extreme study dorks got a slightly late start on Saturday morning. Amy picked out a table with a view of the fountain in the quad.

The table had a catalog for the fall semester lying on top of it. Her dad immediately snatched it up and flipped to the back, ignoring his pancakes. "I don't believe this. Your Dr. Semel went to San Jose State. It doesn't matter how fine a university a professor teaches at, it's where he got his own education that matters. San Jose State is a good school for business, but..." Amy's father shook his head.

"Maybe Dr. Semel's San Jose State teachers all went to Yale," Amy's mother teased gently. She patted Dr. Abbott on the arm. "I'm sure Amy's professor is teaching her everything she needs to know to make up for what she missed in her high school chemistry, Harold."

"He's great," Amy agreed.

"I'd like to meet the man." Her father slapped the catalog closed.

"I don't think he'll be around. Since it's Saturday," Amy explained.

"Well, I want to check out the labs, see the quality of equipment they have you working with."

Amy's mother sent her a *You know your father* look. Amy relaxed enough for her to get down a few bites of her eggs, relieved that she and her mom could still eye-speak—and about her dad!

"And then I think we should take Amy somewhere off this campus," her mother suggested. "I'm sure she'd like a change."

Amy's father grunted as he dug into his pancakes. *Good, a little rudeness,* Amy thought. She got down the rest of her eggs, and the juice.

But relief didn't last long. Soon she was wishing she hadn't coaxed a janitor into letting her dad get a peek at the chemistry lab. The equipment seemed decent enough to Amy, but clearly it was lacking. Her father's expression was more disgusted than when he'd read Dr. Semel's biography.

"Do you know the amount of money I paid to get you into this place? Enough money that you should be working with a brass gram mass set. Much greater accuracy." Dr. Abbott put down the scale he'd been holding. "These tubular spring scales go for about five bucks a pop. And it shows."

Amy and her mother had another eye conversation as Dr. Abbott picked up a cylinder. "Going for economy here, too, I see." He ran his fingernail over the plastic. "This is not suitable for concentrated acids or bases. Or strong solvents, for that matter. What exactly are they having you do in this lab, Amy? Make Play-Doh molecules, for God's sake? If it's anything more complex than that, I shudder to examine the safety equipment. In any case, I'll be making a call to the dean—today."

As she struggled to come up with an answer that could possibly satisfy her father, Amy heard a familiar voice. "Okay if I go in for a minute too? I think I left one of my books." A second later Joel stepped into the room.

"Hey, Amy. I thought I left my chem book in here. Did you see it?" He turned toward her mom and dad. "You must be Amy's parents. She told me you were coming to visit." The Grin made its appearance. "She seemed pretty excited about it."

Amy checked her parents' faces. They bought it. Well, it was sort of true, in a way.

"So you're in this lab too," Dr. Abbott said. "What do you think of the equipment you have to work with?"

"Better than what we have at my high school," Joel answered. "Anyway, this isn't the good stuff. They let us use the level of equipment we need for the experiment we're doing. Guess it saves them money. They end up replacing the cheap equipment more often than the expensive." He tapped the spring scale. "When we get to something where the oil from our fingerprints can screw up our results, they'll pull out the good scales. I'm just waiting to get my hands on the VitroDyne."

Dr. Abbott raised one eyebrow. "Okay," Joel said quickly, "I was showing off. We're not doing anything with the VitroDyne. But they have one in the engineering department, and I met this guy who'll show it to me. They have a video dimensional analyzer, too, so you can get measurement of soft-tissue deformation without contact. Which is so cool."

Whoa, Amy thought. *Joel's inner geek has finally emerged.* Although it was pretty cute the way his blue eyes got all sparkly. It was kinda like when Ephram talked about his anime, or jazz. Except Amy's dad never looked at Ephram the way he was looking at Joel right now.

"So, is your goal to study bioengineering?" Dr. Abbott asked.

"I'm not sure. I absolutely know I want to be a doctor," Joel answered. "I haven't figured out exactly what way I want to do that yet. I'm not sure I'd be happy getting too far away from patients. I'm kind of a people person."

"So am I," Dr. Abbott confided.

Yeah, right, Amy and her mom said to each other in eye-speak.

"Amy, you never mentioned Joel in any of our phone conversations," her dad chided her. "Your mother and I had the impression you were having trouble making friends here."

"Oh my God, kill me now," Amy moaned, turning away.

"We headed to Denver and did some skating in City Park yesterday," Joel said, complete with the Grin, which Amy was starting to hate.

"Really? Wonderful," Amy's dad replied.

He is loving this way, way too much, Amy thought. *Another few seconds, and I'm going to be married to the Grin—and Joel.* "So, thanks for explaining about the equipment. I forgot that's what Ms. Fuller said during the first day of lab," Amy said. That first day Amy had been so miserable that she hadn't retained *anything.* "I'm going to continue giving Mom and Dad the big tour. Maybe we'll see you later."

She grabbed her parents by their elbows and marched them out of there.

Amy walked into Edo Sushi, one parent on either side of her. She wasn't really a sushi girl, but her dad was a sushi man, so this is where the Abbotts always came for dinner when they were in Boulder. At least there were a few non-seaweed choices.

"The first of your party is already here," the hostess told her father.

Oh, no, you didn't, Amy thought. But, oh, yes, he did. Joel was sitting in their booth. With the Grin. He was wearing a suit.

Amy shot her mother a look of betrayal. Was that why she had dragged Amy out shopping this afternoon? Was this why Amy was wearing, at her mother's insistence, a skirt that was too long and a blouse—an actual *blouse*? She'd only agreed to the outfit because she still thought she owed her mother a few. Okay, a couple of hundred. Had she been set up? Had her *mother* fallen in love with Joel too? Amy thought her mother liked Ephram. Well, at least more than her father did.

Mrs. Abbott gave her head a small shake, a shake that said *I knew nothing about this.* Then she smiled at Joel. "So nice you could join us. We hardly got a chance to visit this morning." *She didn't get to be the mayor of Everwood without people skills,* Amy thought.

"Someone's going to have to help me out with the ordering in this place," Joel announced. "I've never had sushi before."

Amy could practically hear her father's heart melting. He loved to be asked for advice. She zoned out as he started giving Joel the history of sushi. *Damage control,* she thought. There was no denying that major damage had been done, and now she desperately needed to get control of the situation. She didn't know Joel that well, but he had to have some unattractive qualities. Was there a way to bring them out without looking like a witch? Because that would be seen as a return to the Amy everyone wanted to forget: the sullen, spoiled, willful, lying, sneaky Amy. She couldn't even remember all the words that had been used to describe her behavior.

But she did know that some words seemed to have been forgotten, like depressed, heartbroken, damaged, mangled. Maybe the words hadn't been totally erased, but she didn't want them as excuses anymore, even if they had been true.

"Amy, the usual tempura?" her father asked, pulling her away from her thoughts.

"Fine. Thanks," she added, not wanting to add "ungrateful" to her list.

But the fact was, she *was* ungrateful. Ungrateful for the presence of Joel, who was only present because her father wanted him there.

"Are you sure you don't want to take another dive in the sushi pool?" Joel asked. "You can't have tried all thirty-two kinds they have here."

"I know what I want to eat, okay?" The words came out sounding harsh. Way harsher than Joel deserved, especially since she'd actually had fun with him yesterday. The first day she'd had fun since she'd arrived in Boulder.

And suddenly Amy realized that she wasn't just ungrateful. She was pissed. But not at Joel—at her father. He knew she was going out with Ephram. But here he was, dragging some guy out to dinner with them just because he was so sure he knew exactly what was right for her. And he was going to make sure she got it. Just like this summer school program—no discussion, just Amy's dad deciding things for her.

"She has very strong feelings about seaweed," Mrs. Abbott explained, basically apologizing for Amy, because clearly Amy couldn't be trusted to do anything on her own.

Amy ate as fast as she could. She excused herself to go to the ladies' room twice. She refused the green-tea ice cream she loved, and managed to guilt everyone else into skipping dessert too.

Finally the monstrosity was over.

Her father stopped the car in front of her dorm. "We'll see you for breakfast," he said stiffly.

"No. No, I want you to come up to my room so I can give you that chemistry textbook," Amy told him. She refused to let the night end without telling him that *his* behavior was unacceptable. "Mom, you should wait in the car. This parking spot isn't legal. You might have to circle the block."

"All right." Her mother clearly understood that Amy had something to say, and she was going to give her the space to say it.

"Amy, it's late. We're all tired," her father protested.

"It'll only take a minute." She got out of the car and waited. A moment later her father's door slammed. They walked toward the dorm in silence. When they were a few feet from the door, she turned to face him. "Dad, I admit that Tommy was a bad choice for me. I admit it took too long for me to see it. I admit that you and Mom were right about him." She pulled in a shaky breath, but managed to keep her voice steady as she continued. "But that doesn't mean . . . have you really decided to pick out the guys I date now?"

"You're exaggerating, Amy," her father said, impatience already creeping into his voice. He always got that tone when you tried to discuss anything with him, as if he'd already heard, thought about, and dismissed everything you could possibly have to say. "I thought it would be nice for you to have a friend at dinner. And I thought Joel might like a little direction on his future plans."

"Bright and I aren't enough for you? You're going to start running the lives of strangers now?" Amy shot back. "And when was the last time you invited one of my friends anywhere? When have you ever invited Ephram to dinner?"

"All right, all right." Her dad held up his hands in mock surrender. "I admit I thought he might be an appropriate boy for you to see. I'm your father.

It's the kind of thing fathers think. It doesn't mean I have a marriage contract in the glove compartment, for crying out loud."

"Can't you just accept the fact that I'm going to keep on making mistakes?" Amy shoved her hair away from her face. "I don't want to, but I am. Maybe about who I'm with. Maybe about other stuff. Everything. But how do you expect me to figure things out if you decide everything for me?"

Her father just looked at her, as if he didn't know what to say.

"It's, like, why we have lab work. The teachers know exactly what's supposed to happen." Maybe her father would get it if she put it in terms that he would understand. "They could just tell us. But they figure we'll learn more if we actually do the experiments and see for ourselves, right?"

"I suppose," her father said. He still sounded impatient, but Amy suspected that this time it was because he knew she was right.

"You've got to let me keep making mistakes." She forced herself to stop talking and give him a chance to respond. It was hard to read his expression in the glow from the dorm's windows. She had no idea what he was going to say.

"The mistakes . . . Amy, we could have lost you." Her father's voice broke. She couldn't see his face, but she could hear the pain behind his words.

"I know. I know." Her eyes began to burn and a

lump formed in her throat. She swallowed it down. She didn't want to start crying. This conversation was too important. "And that's why I need you, you and Mom, so much right now. I think I'll listen to you more than I did last time. I mean, I do realize now that it would have been a good idea to listen to you before."

Amy wiped her eyes with the back of her hand. "I realize something else, too. It would have been a lot easier if I had gone through . . . everything . . . with Tommy if I'd been in my home, with my own room, and my parents, and even my obnoxious brother. Grandma and Irv are great, but I needed my own family."

Her father reached out and pulled her into a tight hug. "We're so glad to have you back."

Amy pulled back so she could look at him. "And not just until I screw up again?"

"No," Dr. Abbott said, in a tone that left no room for doubt. "From now on, I want you doing your experiments from home."

"They're gone," Amy said into her cell.

"He's gone," Ephram answered.

"You know what's weird?" Jennifer shot her a warning look from across the room. Amy lowered her voice. "I sort of miss them."

"I sort of miss him, too—and Delia, but Delia's easy to miss."

Jennifer clicked off the overhead light. "Early class tomorrow," she said pointedly as she climbed into bed.

"Did your dad do the 'I am the Wonderful-and-Yes-Formerly-Famous Dr. Brown'?"

"'Love me. Laugh at my stories. Never look away.' The whole bit. Did your dad do a health inspection of the cafeteria?"

"Almost. And we went to the sushi place. And we had a fight."

"Hey, I had a fight with the Great Dr. Brown. But it turned out decent."

"Mine, too."

"Early class," Jennifer whispered.

"I have to get off now. My roommate needs to sleep. NYC." They'd started saying "NYC" instead of "good-bye." It made it easier—that way they could both hang up thinking of the big New York weekend they had coming up.

"Don't hang up yet," Ephram said quickly. "Just, I don't know, breathe at me for a while."

Amy put the phone next to her on the pillow and drifted off, her breaths getting slower and deeper, falling asleep with Ephram almost beside her.

CHAPTER 6

Ephram's weekly At-A-Glance calendar—a going-away present from Delia—automatically opened to July second, the day that Amy would arrive at Bucks Hollow. She'd only be there for a night and part of the next day, then it was off to New York. He counted the days he had to wait, even though he knew the number he'd come up with: seventeen. And, yep, seventeen was the number he got. Which meant day eighteen, he'd be showing Amy his hometown. Well, maybe more like home-big-city.

It was going to be the perfect weekend. His dad had kicked in a nice amount of cash after Ephram had convinced him the weekend was necessary for jazz music buying and other critical-to-his-musical-success experiences. They didn't need hotel money because they were crashing at his grandparents', and Grandpa Jacob had already gotten them a pair of tickets to see the ballet at Lincoln Center. He kept forgetting the name of the choreographer, but he knew it was someone Russian and famous who was working with an American company for the first time, and that Amy would love it. That was his big surprise for her. And of course he had to take her to Original Ray's—the real one—for pizza, and to Times Square, even though it wasn't nearly as cool now that it had become so sanitized, and Strawberry Fields in the park. And maybe the Cloisters, except it might take too much time, since they only had one weekend, although he was sure Amy would groove on the medieval tapestries, and—

"Heidy-ho." Zoe ambled into his room without knocking, she being Zoe and all, and hoisted herself up onto the corner of his desk. She was wearing socks with the feet cut out on her arms. He didn't bother asking why. He was getting used to the whole New-York-girl odd fashion experiments/statements again. She glanced down at his calendar. "Not too many days to go until G-Day. I get to meet her, right? You know I don't have enough visitors."

"I suppose."

"'I suppose,'" Zoe repeated, imitating his reluctant tone. "The girl will have to eat, Ephram. You can't deny her sustenance." She swung her feet back and forth, tapping out a beat against his metal desk drawer until it bored her. "So, when the library cart came around the practice rooms this morning, I slipped the Johnny boy two cigarettes for some information, and he told me that you, Colorado Ephram Brown, are going in front of the parole board next week, gonna try to convince them to let you play the Tatum, even though the last guy who tried it ended up in the chair."

Ephram tried not to laugh. She loved it too much when she got a laugh. But he couldn't stop a small snort from escaping his nose. "Wait. Did somebody else play jazz for the mid-point recital?"

"Not that I ever heard. Don't be so literal. But if you want someone to go with you to talk to the board, I'm your someone." Zoe had completely dropped the comedy routine. "I'm not passionate about jazz the way you are. But I do believe that we should be able to have a say in what we study here, and I'm happy to tell every teacher and administrator in the place. And you know I think it's your big chance to come out to the Juilliard guys."

"Yeah, that's what I'm gonna argue," Ephram said. "It would be great to have some moral support." Ephram thought he had pulled together a solid argument to present to the board—Ms. Kinney had said that if he got their approval, he could play the Tatum at the final concert. Apparently she didn't want to take the fall all by herself.

But he wasn't sure a great speech would be enough to sway them. "It would help for the board to know that this isn't just about me getting a yes or no on the Tatum. And I'd definitely feel better walking in with you as backup."

"You got me," Zoe promised.

Scritch. Scritch. Scritch. Scritch. Brrrrrt.

And repeat, Amy thought. It's not that Jennifer was making much noise. But the *kind* of noise was driving Amy insane. The sound of the supersharp pencil on paper, then the short burst of the electric pencil sharpener when the pencil got the tiniest bit dull, because Jennifer absolutely could not do equations with a dull pencil. Amy wouldn't mind so much if she could have a little background music, but apparently doing equations with background music was impossible for Amy's neurotic roommate.

Amy couldn't seem to do equations with Jennifer in the room, period. She'd been trying to do her homework for hours and had gotten nowhere. But she couldn't kick her roommate out of her own room.

There was always the library, but Joel might be at the library. He might be at the library with *flowers*. Involuntarily, Amy's eyes slid over to the vase of tulips sitting on her desk. Jennifer caught her. "They're pretty," she commented.

"Yeah." Amy wished they would die. She deliberately hadn't cut off the ends of the stems or put an aspirin in the water to keep the flowers fresh longer, but somehow they were ridiculously healthy. *Don't be such a weenie,* she ordered herself. *You don't want them. Just throw them away already.* She grabbed the aluminum trash can in one hand, the vase in the other, and dumped the tulips, water and all.

"What?" Jennifer asked, pencil halfway to the sharpener.

"Somehow Joel got it in his head that he and I are perfect for each other," Amy burst out. "Probably because my father told him so. But now I've told Joel my dad was out of line, I've told him I have a boyfriend, repeatedly, and he still acts like I'm his girlfriend."

"I guess he really likes you."

Amy snorted. "He likes his big, fat ego. This is all about him not being able to accept the word 'no.'" Amy turned her attention back to her chemistry book. Maybe it would make more sense without those tulips mocking her.

"You ready?" Zoe asked. She had her wild curls restrained in two buns high on her head, and she was wearing a simple skirt—linen, Ephram thought—and a sleeveless white shirt.

"What's with the nun costume?" Ephram asked.

"Hey, gently, gently, catch the monkey. That's what my grandmother says," Zoe replied. "Which basically means that when you want to say something important, don't distract people with clothes they'll think are weird."

"So should I change?" Ephram glanced at his watch. He had enough time before he had to face the board—if he ran.

"Dolly, you've lived in Colorado long enough. You look like an average white boy. You're not going to scare anybody." Zoe patted him on the arm.

Ephram wasn't sure that was a good thing. He didn't need to be scary, exactly, in his meeting with the board. But he wanted to be strong, forceful. He wanted them to see someone who wouldn't back down. Changing into a different shirt wasn't going to give that to him anyway, though. "Okay," he said. "Let's do the Dew. Or just do it. Or some other inspirational phrase created by ad companies." He headed for the entrance to the conference room where all the teachers met weekly to exchange progress reports on their students. He shot a glance through the long windows and saw that Ms. Kinney, Ms. Machado, Mr. Westlake, Mr. Robertson, and Ms. Trussel—a mix of Juilliard and Bucks Hollow faculty—were all sitting behind a polished wooden table.

"Oooh, it's so *Flashdance*. I may have to break

out into my combo of ballet and erotic dancing," Zoe exclaimed.

"Oooh, I might have to leave you outside."

"You've never seen it, have you?" she asked.

Ephram shook his head.

"Well, I rented the DVD a couple of dozen times during my review of the culture of the eighties. And you're Jennifer Beals, fighting for the chance to do what you love." Zoe hesitated. "Except it didn't turn out that great for her in the scene I was thinking of, but never mind. You always knew Jennifer went on and danced the way she wanted to. And so will you."

"Are you finished?" Ephram nodded at the closed door. "Because we're here."

"After you," Zoe said. Ephram rubbed his face with his hands, then straightened his shoulders, and entered the room. Every eye turned toward him. He forced a smile onto his face and walked what felt like a mile and a half over to the table.

"Sit down, sit down," said Ms. Trussel, director of the Bucks Hollow camp, trying to make it sound as if she were welcoming them into her living room. She didn't exactly pull it off, but Ephram and Zoe sat.

"You didn't tell me you were bringing a friend, Ephram," Ms. Kinney commented. Her face did not show a lot of expression. She was good at that.

"I'm not here as a friend," Zoe answered. "I'm here as a concerned student. I think today's decision is a precedent-making one."

Ephram stared at her. Zoe hadn't just switched up her clothes; her attitude had gotten a makeover too. Her words came out crisp and cool. Ephram suddenly felt like he had an attorney sitting beside him. What other people did Zoe have buried inside of her?

"Are you saying *you* want to change the piece you're playing for the final concert?" asked Mr. Robertson, Zoe's teacher, his voice rising.

"No, Mike, what I'm saying is that the faculty and administrators need to see the students preparing for college as what they are: nearly adults—people who should be allowed to make their own decisions about their future." Ms. Kinney opened her mouth to speak, but Zoe held up one finger to silence her. "With guidance, of course. But the ultimate decisions, good or bad, should be our own, because it is *our* future."

Ephram was still distracted by Zoe calling her teacher by his first name. He didn't even know what Ms. Kinney's first name was—and the idea of using it . . . He shoved the thoughts away. It was time to take control. This was his meeting, and he needed to show his stuff.

"I know you're all aware of the history of jazz," he began, hoping the opening to his speech didn't sound as rehearsed as it felt, "and of Art Tatum's part in that history. You know the technical difficulty involved in playing his pieces, the tempo changes, the fill-ins, the full-keyboard runs. Developing the dexterity alone is an accomplishment. And any scout from Juilliard—or any other school—will know that."

"Ephram, I've never said that playing a Tatum piece is easy." Ms. Kinney rested both of her hands, palms down, on the shiny wooden table. "What I've said is that our admissions scouts from Juilliard are conservative. They are going to respond more favorably to a classical piece. The Bach we've been working on is an ideal showcase for you, and I can guarantee you it's your best shot at getting accepted to the school. You can't tell me that isn't what you want." She stared directly at him, her blue eyes issuing a challenge.

"I want a school that values my passion." Ephram was on his feet without knowing exactly when he'd stood up. "I have that for the Tatum. I don't for the Bach. It shows in my playing. Are the scouts from Juilliard so conservative that they don't love music anymore? That they won't recognize it in someone else and say, 'That's who I want at my school'? Someone who feels music in his guts and his balls, not just in his head and his hands?"

He sat down, realizing he had just said "balls" in

front of the board. That hadn't been part of the speech. But damn it, that's what he wanted them to understand.

"It's not that I don't think they'd appreciate your . . . enthusiasm," Ms. Trussel said. "It's just that they're—"

"They're old," Mr. Robertson jumped in.

"Not all of them," Ms. Kinney protested. "It's not about age. It's about—"

"I know for a fact that one of the Juilliard scouts who will be at the final concert smokes pot," Zoe interrupted, her voice still lettuce-leaf crisp. "Another one was arrested in college for public indecency. These people aren't so conservative. They live in New York City," she finished, pronouncing the name of the city slowly, as if she were speaking to five-year-olds.

"Maybe some of them are actually tired of hearing Bach," Ephram jumped in. "I personally could listen to a well-played Bach sonata forever." He decided a little sucking up couldn't hurt. Even though when he played Bach, he felt like a robot pounding out some mechanical tune. "But if I went from audition to audition, listening to it over and over, I might get tired of it."

"And if Ephram's wrong about the Tatum, so what?" Zoe asked, dropping her lawyer-girl attitude. "More room for the rest of us!"

He shot her a look. She gave him a big smile.

"Do you have anything else you want to say?" Ms. Trussel asked Ephram.

Should he have more to say? Was he supposed to have more to say? Was she saying he hadn't said enough?

"Just that I think it should be my choice. And I'm ready to accept the consequences—good or bad."

Ms. Trussel nodded. "Let us talk alone for a few minutes, then we'll let you know our decision."

Ephram walked out of the room, hoping the line of sweat in the middle of his back hadn't soaked through his shirt—'cause that would sort of screw with the final impression he wanted to make.

"So what'd ya think?" Zoe asked the second she closed the door behind her. "Was I brilliant, or what? I know. I was brilliant."

"I hope that they got that the way I feel about the Tatum shows in how I play. That's the most important thing I wanted them to understand."

"Uh-uh." Zoe tugged at the collar of her shirt as if it was annoying her. "The most important thing we had to get across was that the Juilliard scouts aren't as conservative as everyone is so afraid they are. I totally nailed that with the pot and the public indecency thing."

Ephram leaned against the side of the mansion. It was still warm, even though the sky was starting to darken. He felt like he'd just run a race. Not that he often ran races, but when forced to in gym, he'd ended up with this same limp-legged feeling, and all he'd done was walk into a room, say some stuff, and walk out.

"I wonder if these Bucks Hollow people go into the city for anything but concerts," Zoe continued. "And the professors who are actually here from Juilliard? How conservative can you be, surrounded by—"

Ms. Kinney swung open the door. She smiled at Ephram, a closed-mouth, fake-looking smile. "The board's decided. It's your choice what you play, Ephram. I hope you'll think it over."

"I'm playing the Tatum," he answered immediately. He'd done all the thinking he needed to do.

Ms. Kinney nodded, unsurprised, and disappeared back inside. Zoe let out a "Yeah!" way too loud to have come out of such a small body. "Let's go."

She took off down the cobblestone path.

"Go where?" Ephram asked, following her. When she walked fast like this, you had to follow her. Somehow she made it clear that it was expected of you.

"Back to my room to celebrate my victory!"

"*Your* victory?" Ephram teased.

"Mine, ours, whoever's. I've got champagne. It's pink, unfortunately, and it'll be warm, but it's better than nothing."

"No can do. I've got to start working the Tatum

full out tomorrow. Hungover and riffs? Wouldn't be pretty," Ephram said. "But you *were* great in there."

"Wuss." Zoe opened the door to her room and pushed him inside. "Anyway, it's not about the champagne. It's about the celebrating. Just have a sip. You can use my toothbrush glass." She ducked into the bathroom and returned with a bottle and a glass. "Can you believe it's screw-top?" she asked as she twisted open the cap of the champagne and poured some into the glass. "I didn't rinse it, so you'll get a minty kick. Yum." She took a swig straight from the bottle, then plopped down on her bed.

Ephram sprawled on the floor and took a sip of Zoe's concoction. It was pretty awful. "Did you see Kinney's face when she had to tell me I had permission? It was like, like . . . she just had a slug of this." Ephram pointed to the glass.

"Wasn't the info on the Juilliard scouts I got amazing?" Zoe yanked off her shirt. She had a little tank top on underneath. She didn't seem aware that she was kind of stripping down in front of a guy. "I know a cool alum, and I got the indecent exposure thing off the Internet. I am a genius!"

"I'll drink to that. But without really drinking. That stuff is noxious. And the toothpaste didn't help." Ephram took his cell phone out of his jacket pocket and set it next to him. Amy usually called around now, and he wanted to be sure to hear the ring.

"Yeah, it's gross." Zoe set the bottle on her nightstand. "I gave one of the gardeners a twenty. I knew we were in big trouble when I saw the amount of change I got back. But it was too late. Hey, did you like my voice of authority? I was going for a sort of Connie Chung meets Judge Judy."

"It worked—"

"And I think the outfit had an effect, even if it was just subliminal. And the mention of the city. Even when people say they'd never want to live there, it's intimidating when you bring up people who do. And really, how can these Connecticut dwellers actually know what a Manhattanite thinks is conservative? I wonder how many of our Juilliard profs are actually NYC born-and-bred." Zoe jumped to her feet. "I'll get out my laptop! I can show you the whole article I found on the indecent exposure."

A night of reliving Zoe's greatest hits, Ephram thought as he stood up. *No thanks. Pretty soon she'll have forgotten I was even at the meeting with her.* "I'm gonna head out."

"What, no thank-you?" Zoe called after him.

That chemical compound looks kind of like Ephram holding a golf club, Amy thought. *Or maybe Ephram with kind of a horse's leg.* She shook her head. Clearly she missed her boyfriend, but she needed to focus. Even though Dr. Semel went to San Jose State, it wasn't likely he would ask her to identify compounds by the way they resembled Ephram Brown.

When did studying become so hard? She used to be like Jennifer. Well, at least she'd been able to hit the books for hours at a time. Now she had the attention span of a two-year-old. If someone held up a set of keys and jangled them, she'd probably stare for hours. A chemistry book, not so much. After ten minutes, the words and symbols faded to gray.

A knock on the door immediately drew her attention. The door swung open before either she or Jennifer could call "Come in," and there stood Joel and the Grin. "I brought supplies for my study monkeys," Joel announced. He had started sucking up to Jennifer, and she totally loved it. "Caffeine in the form of diet soda. Brain food in the form of peanuts. Physical satisfaction in the form of chocolate—although I could be convinced to give back rubs."

Jennifer giggled. Amy shook her head. "What syllable of 'boyfriend' didn't you understand, Joel?"

Joel sat down next to Amy on her bed. "You told me about one of your boyfriends yourself. A dealer and a user."

Jennifer had lowered her head over one of her books, but Amy caught her roommate's eyes widening in shock. "Thanks," she mouthed to Joel, tilting her head toward Jennifer.

"Oh, she understands," Joel said. "Jennifer's had some experience with bad boys, I bet." Jennifer blushed. He turned back to Amy. "I just think you should be with someone who's going to be really good to you, take care of you. For example, someone who has gotten tickets for a revival of *The Red Shoes* on Saturday, which I happen to know is one of your favorite movies and you've never been able to see it on the big screen."

"Ephram is great. I love him. Which is why, no, Joel, I will not be going to the movies with you." *Wait*, Amy thought. *Did I just say I love Ephram?* It was the first time she'd used the word. She'd just told Ephram that she "more than liked" him. But the love word came out so easily. It was true. She did love him, from the deepest part of herself.

Joel peeled open a candy bar and held it out to her, apparently oblivious to the fact that she had just repeatedly rejected him.

Amy pushed it away. "You know what? You've got to go now. I'm calling Ephram. Most nights we fall asleep on the phone, so there's no point in waiting." Amy hit her speed dial. Ephram's name came up on her cell's screen. She smiled at it.

"Ephram's phone," a girl said in her ear. "Zoe here. Speak to me."

Shocked, Amy hit the END button. She stared at

the phone as if it were some sort of poisonous creature.

"Nice." The Grin made its biggest appearance yet. "A girl just answered your boyfriend's phone."

Joel knew a great exit line, and he used it, leaving Amy alone to hear that girl's voice in her head over and over again.

She returned to studying. She had to. Midterms were on Monday, and she had to nail them. There was no other option. It wouldn't erase the past few months—nothing would—but this was a start. A way to begin to prove herself.

But that voice. She kept hearing that voice in her head. *"Zoe here. Speak to me." "Zoe here. Speak to me."* Why had a girl answered Ephram's phone? Why did she sound like she had every right to? Why was her name *Zoe*?

Finally, all Amy could do was roll over on her side, face the wall, put her pillow on her head, and try to sleep. Sleep would reset her brain. She wasn't delusional. She didn't expect to wake up with no memory of Zoe Whoever. But she thought maybe she would gain a little perspective.

Unfortunately that was so not the case. The questions had only multiplied and permutated in Amy's brain overnight. They distracted her from the morning's lecture, so she didn't have even her usual hole-filled notes to fill in at lunch. And then she burned her finger during lab lighting a Bunsen burner, something she'd done successfully a dozen times this summer.

She took a walk to try to clear her head. She ate some dinner—not that she could remember what she'd eaten a minute after she'd dumped her tray. She even talked to Ephram—but couldn't quite force a question about Zoe out of her mouth. But Ephram sounded like Ephram. And that was a good thing. So when she sat down at her desk to study, she was sure that she'd be able to . . . study.

"Zoe here. Speak to me." "Zoe here. Speak to me."

Like chemistry wasn't hard enough to understand already without that garbage churning around in her head.

All day.

All night.

Until she couldn't take it. She grabbed her cell phone and dialed.

"Joel? Did you find anyone to go to *The Red Shoes* with? Because I'm going to go insane if I don't get out of here."

"Ephram, wait up. I found the perfect thing for you and your country girl to do in the city." Zoe caught up to him as he headed down the row of practice rooms. There was no set schedule for after dinner, but he was hoping to get in at least another hour or so on the Tatum.

"There's this guy who pierces himself with these

long, really thin needles, then he has someone hang limes from the needles, so the weight pulls down on them."

"The point being?" Ephram checked the rooms. They were all full. He shook his head. Did everyone in this place practice compulsively? Were they all taking Ritalin with their oatmeal?

"I thought you were a jazz man. I thought you wouldn't need an interpretation." Zoe didn't look happy with him. "It's kind of like an Indian rite of passage. Native, not Eastern. But maybe you and Small Town would rather go to Serendipity and share a frozen hot chocolate. It's right down the block from Bloomie's, you know."

Ephram no longer had any trouble keeping from laughing while talking to Zoe. She was so in love with herself, he was surprised she even bothered talking to other people at all. "You know what, I actually need to call Small Town," he said. He sat down in one of the chairs at the end of the hall, pulled out his cell, and waited for Zoe to leave. It took her a couple of seconds too long to get the message, but she finally did, and he was alone at last. He hit speed dial one on his cell. Amy's voice mail came on. He hit speed dial two.

"Hello?" Amy's roommate said.

"Jennifer, hey. It's Ephram. Is Amy there?"

"She's at the movies with Joel. Can I take a message?"

"No." Ephram struggled to take a breath. "Um, no thanks. Forget I called, okay?" He clicked his cell shut. He stared at the door of his practice room down the hall, but there was no way he could think about the Tatum now.

Joel. That's who he was thinking about.

"Every time Vicky dances out of the theater in those red toe shoes, I know what's going to happen and it's still so horrible." Amy pulled in a breath of the crisp air, refreshingly clean after the stale-popcorn smell of the revival movie house.

"So you're glad you came out?" Joel held up her sweater so she could slide her arms in.

"Yes. This was the perfect thing. That story always gets to me." Amy had gotten completely absorbed in seeing it played out on a big screen for the first time. She'd made Joel sit all the way up front, so the screen filled almost her entire field of vision, the soundtrack almost too loud in her ears. For a few hours there was no Zoe. Or Joel, even though he was sitting right beside her. Or Dr. Semel. Or confusing hole-filled notes, or unfinished chemistry problems, or upcoming midterms. There wasn't even any Ephram. Or any Amy.

"*You* always get to me." Joel gently turned Amy to face him, then leaned down, moving in for a kiss. All at once the reality of her life rushed back to her. Zoe, Ephram, Dr. Semel, all of it.

"No." Amy stepped back. "Sorry. This was wrong of me." She gathered her long hair into a ponytail, then released it. "Joel, I totally used you tonight. I said I'd come to the movies with you, but nothing's really changed with me. I love Ephram. I just . . ."

"Needed a study break?" Joel offered.

"No." Amy decided to go for honesty. She figured he deserved it. "Hearing that girl answer Ephram's phone, it made me psycho. I didn't think I was the psycho type. I couldn't stop thinking about it. I guess I wanted to know that I could have someone else too, if I wanted. Stupid. Immature. Again, sorry."

Joel shook his head. "Not many chicks could get me to see an old ballerina movie. Remember that."

He walked her home, and didn't try to kiss her again when he got there. Amy went inside feeling terrible. She'd probably just managed to alienate the one and only friend she had made all summer.

She decided it was too late for any studying that night. But she had all day Sunday. She set the alarm for five A.M., and actually got up when it rang—no snooze button. Then, two cups of coffee balanced on her notebooks, she hit the study lounge with the surprisingly large number of kids already down there. *You can do this,* she told herself. And she could. She'd certainly gotten A's on tests before after one good day of cramming.

• • •

Not this time, though.

This time she got a C on the written and a B-minus on the practical.

She needed a B minimum to get into the AP physics class in the fall, which was the whole point of the summer session, of her dad pulling the strings.

She wasn't cutting it. She couldn't even imagine the look on her father's face when he . . . no, that wasn't true. She could imagine the look in every detail, because she had disappointed him so often lately.

And now she was disappointing him again. How had this happened? How had she lost the ability to study, to think, to *learn*?

I have to ace the final—both parts, Amy told herself. *And I will.*

She wouldn't allow herself to consider any other possibility. But the question was, how?

Ephram sat down on the piano bench. Mid-point concert. Just a little preview of what the representatives from Juilliard and the other schools would hear in another month. He closed his eyes—Tatum was pretty much blind, maybe it would inspire him—and started to play.

Crap. Crap, crap, crap. That's all his stuttering brain could come up with. Ephram couldn't pinpoint exactly what was wrong—it was just stiff. Too slow on that run, too fast on the next. The Tatum piece sometimes went almost entirely with the harmony, but Ephram felt as if he'd lost the melody completely. *Crap*.

Each time he realized he'd made a mistake, he made another one. People said that when Art Tatum played, sometimes the audience thought they were hearing two pianos. That could be happening to his audience too. They could think they were hearing two very crappy pianos.

Finally it was over. He stood up and spotted Ms. Kinney in the audience before anyone else. She didn't look triumphant. She actually looked like she felt bad for him.

But Ephram could tell she was thinking that she'd been right all along. He was pretty sure every single person in the auditorium was thinking the same thing. And he half agreed with them himself. Half? Make that ninety percent.

He was a terrible pianist whose girlfriend might be cheating on him.

This was the worst summer ever.

CHAPTER 7

Ephram sat through the rest of the concert, his own failed performance playing in his head over and over during every piece. Then he got out of there as quickly as possible, which wasn't really all that quickly. Getting out of there involved stopping to speak to Ms. Kinney, and agreeing that the Tatum needed more work. Congratulating Zoe on her Mendelssohn. Congratulating Greg, who had actually managed to do a passable job on his Schubert. Smiling at Ms. Trussel. Congratulating, congratulating, even being congratulated by a parent who obviously didn't know jazz, until he was out of the auditorium. Then it was only a short distance to his room—a few more smiles, a few more congratulations to give, none to accept, thank God. And he was alone. It was over.

Except for the call.

His dad was expecting him to call in with a report. He'd gotten himself so invested in Ephram playing jazz that now he wanted daily updates. And the mid-point recital was the biggest news so far. How humiliating to have to admit that he'd blown it. He'd gotten so distracted by Joel—whoever he was—that he'd ruined his recital.

Ephram decided he had about ten minutes to lick his wounds—gross image—then he'd have to call. Ten minutes to just—

His cell rang. Ephram looked at the phone, as if he didn't know who it was going to be. "I was gonna call you," he muttered. He considered not answering, but decided it was better to get it over with. The ripping-off-the-Band-Aid theory. "Hey, Dad."

"So? How'd it go?"

Ephram took a deep breath. "I sucked."

"I think I need a translation of that, Ephram," Dr. Brown said. "Does that mean you made some mistakes that a professional would notice, or—"

"You could hear actual sucking sounds coming out of the piano," Ephram said. "Bad notes, bad transitions. No rhythm. Short, polite applause afterward. My teacher looked ready to puke."

"What happened?"

Of course the Great Dr. Brown would like a nice, clear explanation. Something he could fix. Something he could tell one of his inspirational tales about.

"Ephram?"

And the great doctor wanted the nice explanation with no pause for thinking. Ephram sighed. He knew the reason. And he knew his father wasn't going to like it. But what else could he say? Ripping off the Band-Aid.

"It was Amy," he admitted. "When I called her over the weekend, her roommate told me she was out with some guy. I couldn't stop thinking about it. I tried to practice, but I just . . . I just kept thinking about *Joel*."

"I see. Did you bring it up with Amy?" Ephram could almost picture the expression on his father's craggy face. His eyebrows would be pulled together, and his eyes would be looking at Ephram as if he were the only thing in the world at that moment.

"No," Ephram muttered. He knew he should have. But when he'd actually talked on the phone with Amy, he hadn't been able to figure out how to work it in without sounding like a jealous freak. And on some level, he didn't want to ask her about Joel. Because what if she said she was seeing this guy? How could Ephram deal with that?

"Well, it might not be a bad idea to discuss your fears with Amy," his dad said. "But, you know, there's always going to be something distracting you when you have to play in front of an audience. No one has a life without distractions."

Ephram waited for his father to launch into a story about one of his groundbreaking brain surgeries, but he didn't. "Part of growing up is figuring out how to deal with those distractions—whether you're playing the piano, or performing surgery, or reading to your daughter."

Ephram had to admit, the phone call was going better than he'd expected. "Ah, the wise old Dr. Brown," he teased.

"I'm serious," his father protested.

"So, do you have any advice for getting over my crushing humiliation?" Ephram asked.

"Well, last time *I* was stressed, Nina was too busy to talk me down, so she sent me home with some of her bubble bath."

Ephram pulled the phone away from his ear for a moment, then reluctantly returned it. "You just gave me an image I didn't need to have."

"You'll figure out your own way of dealing."

"That's it? You don't want to do some yelling or anything?"

"Nope. But I'll be at the final concert. You aren't planning on screwing up while I'm there, are you?"

"Ass."

"See you in a few weeks." His father hung up.

Ephram smiled.

"What are you going to Connecticut for?" the blond woman sitting next to Amy asked. The woman looked kind of like Madison, Ephram's first real girlfriend—first real *love.* Amy didn't even like to think about what else Madison had been to him.

"Um, I'm going to visit my boyfriend. He's in a piano program there. A serious one. For students who are working at concert level." Amy couldn't believe she'd just hurled out all that information. She wasn't so much the talking-to-people-she-didn't-know type. She'd rather just read.

"How long has it been since you've seen him?" The woman clearly liked to talk. And when Amy took a closer look, she realized it was only the hair that was anything like Madison's. The rest of her features were completely different. *I've got to get out of this jealous haze,* she thought. *If the Zoe thing was such a big deal, I should have talked to Ephram about it. But I didn't, and I can't bring it up now, so much later. So it's done.*

"Not that long. About a month," Amy answered.

"But that can feel like a long time. You must be excited."

"Uh-huh." Amy tried to make the answer come out sleepy. She closed her eyes. She didn't want to talk the whole way there. Especially because she thought the woman might eventually figure out that Amy wasn't as excited as she "must be."

I'll see Ephram, and everything will be all right, she promised herself. And she almost believed it.

"Uh-oh. What did you do?"

It took Ephram a minute to realize that the

thirtysomething guy in the baseball hat was talking to him. "What'd I do?" he repeated.

The baseball-hat guy pointed to the roses Ephram held. The crisp plastic wrapping was making his hand sweat. "Those aren't flowers for screwing up? They're the kind I always buy when my wife goes to visit her sister for a while because she can't stand the sight of me. You bought them from the kid on the meridian right before you turn into the parking lot, right?"

"Yeah. But I just thought my girlfriend would like them. We didn't—she's coming in so we can spend the weekend in New York. She's never been there before. I'm taking her to the ballet." Ephram didn't know why he was explaining so much to Baseball Hat, but he really wanted the guy to know that everything was great between him and Amy.

Because it was. So she'd gone to a movie with Joel, whoever Joel was. It's not like Ephram expected her to only speak to girls the whole time she was in Boulder. A movie was just a movie. Sitting in the dark. Close together. By themselves.

If it was that big of a deal to you, you should have asked her about it, Ephram told himself. It was too late now. He would sound crazy if he dragged up something from a week ago.

"The ballet, huh?" Baseball Hat said. "No wonder you don't seem excited."

"I'm excited. I'm completely excited." *Or I will*

be as soon as I see Amy, he thought. He wished he could be right there the second she stepped off the plane, but the baggage carousel was the closest he could get. He headed over to the drinking fountain just to get away from the baseball-hat guy, who was giving him the creeps. Ephram was still bent over the arc of water when he heard Amy's voice.

"Hey."

He straightened up and turned around in one sharp, awkward motion, a little water dribbling down his chin. He wiped it away with the back of his hand. "Hey."

"We got in early—"

"Sorry I wasn't looking—"

They both stopped talking. "You first," Amy said.

"Um, these are for you." He thrust the flowers out, just as Amy was stepping in to hug him. Ephram froze, embarrassed. He'd gotten flower-water all over her shirt. Amy wiped it off, then gave him a little half-hug.

It was like the Tatum all over again. Nothing felt right. The rhythm was off. At least they managed to kiss, and nothing could completely screw that up.

"So first Bucks Hollow, and then the Big Apple." *I sound like a tour guide. I should be wearing a blazer,* Ephram thought.

"Sounds good!" Amy chirped. She never chirped. It sounded weird, not Amy-like.

"Okay, um. Let's go." It didn't even occur to him

to take Amy's bag until he noticed her struggling to drag it through the crowd. And when he finally took it from her it seemed like too little, too late.

When was he going to start feeling excited? Amy was standing right in front of him . . . and all he felt was the distance between them.

This is just as bad as my school, Amy thought. Although, Bucks Hollow was beautiful. The grounds looked like they required a constant crew to keep them at such a level of perfection. And the mansion that had been converted into the school itself—well, there was nothing like it in Everwood. But no one was around to enjoy it. As far as Amy could tell, everyone was locked up somewhere, working. Ephram was shut away in his little practice room, doing battle with the Tatum.

Amy sat down on one of the stone benches scattered artfully here and there under the trees. *Am I the first person to ever sit down here?* she wondered as she pulled her copy of *Life of Pi* out of her straw bag. Amy knew she should be using this time to study, but she couldn't deal with the Ephram weirdness. Because there was definitely weirdness—they'd hardly been able to manage a decent hug, let alone any chemistry.

Clearly she couldn't deal with reading about a zoo in India either, because she had read the same few paragraphs of her book at least four times, and still all she knew was that there were animals involved. Amy sighed and stuck the book back in her bag. She needed to find Ephram. Maybe if she just watched him practice, just stood there and soaked up some Ephram essence, she'd feel better. Maybe she'd feel less like she was about to spend the whole weekend with a stranger.

It didn't take Amy long to track down Ephram's practice room. She quietly pulled open the door, about to whisper that she just wanted to listen. The words evaporated when she saw another girl sitting in the room's one chair. Ephram wasn't working at all. He was hanging out, talking to a girl—an adorable, petite girl who looked kind of like an elf. Amy wanted to smash her little elf head in. *Smash her head in?* She'd never wanted to smash anyone's head in before in her life.

"Ames, hey," Ephram said. "This is Zoe. She's heard about you pretty much every day."

"Seriously," said the tiny elf girl, rolling her big brown eyes.

"She just came in 'cause she's having problems with her Mendelssohn and wanted to talk it through."

All Amy heard was the name *Zoe.* The elf girl was Zoe. From the phone. *"This is Zoe. Speak to me."* That Zoe. Zoe stuck out her hand. "He never shuts up about you. It's really annoying," she said cheerfully. "You and your big trip to Manhattan. That's where I'm from, by the way. I tried to hook you up with a show, but Ephram didn't think you'd like it."

Amy finally realized Zoe's hand was out there for her to shake. She grabbed it. Zoe had a firm grip, not the limp girly kind. "What *do* you want to do on your weekend?" Zoe asked.

"Ephram's been making the plans—he's the expert. All I know for sure is I want to go to the top of the Empire State Building."

There was a brief, awkward silence.

"I guess that's kind of dorky," Amy said. "You New Yorkers have probably been there a million times."

"Actually, no. I've never been," Zoe said. "It's a flyover thing. I bet Ephram's never gone either." Zoe turned to him.

Ephram ran his fingers through his hair, making it stand up more than usual. "Nope."

"What do you mean, 'flyover'?" Amy asked.

"States you fly over getting from New York to California. You're from Ohio. That's a flyover," Zoe explained.

The air in the little room started to heat up. But the warmth of an extra body shouldn't be making a change so fast, should it? Regardless of whatever was making the temperature rise, Amy felt little dewdrops of perspiration starting to form along her hairline. "I'm from Colorado."

"Whatever." Zoe gave a dismissive flap of her hand.

"You're the girl who answered Ephram's cell phone, aren't you?" Amy asked Zoe the question, but she locked her eyes on Ephram's face.

"What?" Ephram seemed to actually be surprised.

"Was that you?" Zoe asked.

"Why was she answering your phone, Ephram? It was really late."

"Who is Joel and why were you at the movies with him last Saturday night?" Ephram stood up so fast he almost knocked the piano bench over.

"Okay, that's my cue. See you guys later." Zoe slipped out of the room, closing the door firmly behind her.

"Joel's this guy who was my lab partner a couple of times. I was going crazy sitting in my dorm room. I had to get out of there for a little while. Was I supposed to ask your permission?" Amy demanded.

"Amy, we talk every day. You never mentioned the guy's name. That tells me something."

This room was way too small. Amy didn't want to be having this conversation with Ephram so close. But there was no choice. "And you talked to me about Zoe all the time, right?" she snapped. "Clearly you're friends with her, and you've never even said her name to me."

Ephram threw up his hands. "I don't talk about her because I get more than enough of her. She annoys the hell out of me. She latched onto me the first day because I was from New York. At first it was cool to talk to her about some of the places where I used to hang. But that's almost *all* she wants to talk about. That or how great she is. And she's bossy as hell. I left my cell phone in her room one time because I wanted to get out of there so bad I forgot it."

Amy was stunned. That tiny elf girl was a bossy monster?

She laughed. There was no way Ephram was lying. He couldn't lie that well. After a second, he laughed too. "How embarrassing," he said. "Terrorized by a little girl."

Amy sat down in the chair. "You want to know the entire truth about Joel?"

Ephram nodded.

"He tells everyone he's pre-premed, as if that even exists. He has an ego the size of Boulder. And of course, my dad loved him. So Joel got the idea that my father thought he was the perfect guy for me, and when I told him I already had a boyfriend his massive ego kicked in. He had to win me, or something like that, mostly to prove he could."

"But why the movies?"

"I was pissed off that a girl had answered your cell," Amy admitted. "I should have asked you about it, but it always felt like the wrong time. Even though I thought about it constantly. So I wanted some distraction. Or maybe I wanted to get back at you. Anyway, I ended up treating Joel badly. And you. Nothing happened, but I shouldn't have gone."

Ephram didn't say anything. He just sank back down onto the piano bench and laced his fingers behind his neck. He smiled at her.

"What?" Amy asked.

"You know what this was?" he said. "This was our first fight."

"We've had fights before. Big, ugly fights," Amy reminded him.

"I meant our first couple fight," he told her. "And it wasn't that bad."

Amy thought about it, a reluctant smile tugging at her lips. "You're right. It was only like a three."

"I'd give it a two point five." Ephram patted the piano bench next to him, and Amy moved over to sit there. "This is a big deal. The first couple fight." He brushed her hair away from her face, and she turned toward him, just as he leaned in to kiss her. She kissed him back, then gazed up at him happily.

"I'm glad it's over," she said.

"Me too. And now that it *is* over, our trip to New York is going to be perfect."

"This is so normal. Real people actually live here. I mean I knew that, but . . ." Amy looked around, taking in the mom with the baby stroller, the people eating at a sidewalk café, the Gap, Barnes & Noble.

"You're now seeing the non-touristy New York," Ephram agreed. "The Upper West Side. Scoffed at by some as too tame, but, you know, not everyone can have their very own crackhead living in their lobby."

"Or swarms of half-dressed girls screeching outside their windows?"

"That's definitely a Times Square thing. MTV's always filming something there. And when you got cameras, you got the chicks. If you'd stripped down a little like I advised, you could have been on—"

Amy elbowed him in the ribs. "It was worth seeing. Those little kids dancing were amazing. And that preacher who said bar codes were a sign of the apocalypse—truly enlightening."

Ephram nodded. "I usually avoid Times Square, but I guess it does have its charms. The Disney theater two blocks away from a triple-X movie theater and a block away from a revival of an Edward Albee play—kind of mind-blowing."

"Plus, lots of seminaked girls for my boyfriend to enjoy," Amy added.

"I wasn't—," Ephram protested.

"It was like drinking ten cups of coffee. While this"—Amy gestured to the strolling people, and outdoor diners—"is more like one Frappuccino."

"Here it is: Zabars." Ephram led the way inside.

Amy was hit by hundreds of smells—salty, sweet, pungent, spicy, sour. . . . The inside of her nose tickled, her mouth watered, and she didn't know where to look first.

"Cheese. We need cheese." Ephram sounded like an overexcited little kid—so not Ephram. He grabbed Amy's hand and tugged her through a maze of aisles and over to a massive, waist-high glass case stocked with more kinds of cheese than Amy knew existed. More cheeses hung from the ceiling—along with, strangely, a pair of dark brown wooden clogs—and the shelves behind the case were stacked with more. They ranged in color from a delicate white to a very deep orange.

Ephram and Amy got in line. "I think some Parmigiano-Reggiano, and some Danish Blue. I know the blue is mold. But I can't help it. I love it. What do you want, Ames?"

"I guess cheddar or Swiss isn't the kind of answer you're looking for." Amy's eyes darted from cheese to cheese.

"The only reason I know anything about the *fromage* is that Nonny is a fanatic about it. You want to do bread and dessert?"

"Absolutely." She left him with the cheeses and wandered around until she saw bread hanging from the ceiling. The bread counter was a smaller, less overwhelming version of the cheese counter, and Amy managed it with no real problems, although her head was feeling overstuffed with names—old-fashioned Jewish rye bread, sourdough *ficelles,* semolina bread, Eli's Raisin Pecan Rolls, onion rolls, pumpernickel, raisin pumpernickel, Manor House breads, brioche rolls, health bread, seven-grain, heavy whole wheat . . . and that didn't include all the types of bagels. Or croissants.

And this is the world Ephram came from, Amy thought, heading over to the glass case filled with desserts. A world filled with choices about everything. Not just food, but wildly different neighborhoods. And people, and schools, and entertainment. In Everwood, it was the high-school production of *Into the Woods* or nothing. When Ephram came back to this city after graduation—because Juilliard would take him, she knew that—would he ever be satisfied living anywhere else again?

"Can I help you?" a tall guy in a white apron and a yellow Zabars baseball cap asked.

"My boyfriend is from here, but now he lives in Colorado. So what kind of dessert would he want, do you think?"

"No question about it, black-and-white cookies," the guy said. He pointed to a tray of giant cookies, each half-covered with vanilla icing and half-covered with chocolate.

"I'll take a dozen," Amy told him. She doubted

even Ephram could eat that many at their picnic, but this way he could take some back to school. She spotted him over at a deli counter, and began the slow process of making her way over there. Too many people. Amy wasn't feeling like she was on one Frappuccino anymore. There were some espressos added in. The buzz was exciting, but she wouldn't want to be buzzing all the time. Which meant that she couldn't really see herself living in Ephram's city.

"So are you finally going to tell me the location of our secret picnic?" Amy asked as she and Ephram combined their supplies and paid for them.

"We can walk there from here," Ephram said.

New Yorkers seemed to walk as much as people who lived in Colorado. They just walked in different settings. New Yorkers didn't put on their hiking boots and hit the trails; they hit the sidewalks and walked to the stores or movies, or museums, or walked from the subways to work. The sidewalks were never empty—or quiet. In some ways, stepping onto an NYC sidewalk was like stepping into a river. The tide of people just pulled you along. "It's like you get a fresh burst of energy every time you step out into the street," Amy commented.

"Yeah. I never really realized that until I left here. I thought every place was like this." Ephram's eyes sparkled. He kept turning his head, as if he wanted to soak in *everything*. "Let's cut over to the park."

"Picnic destination?"

Ephram smiled. "No. Just an interesting way to get where we're going. The great thing about summer is it won't get dark for hours, so we don't have to worry."

They turned the corner, and immediately Central Park came into sight. Amy had seen it from Ephram's grandparents' apartment, but she was still amazed at how huge it was. The first thing she saw when they stepped into the park was a homeless woman asleep on one of the benches, covered by a down coat and a dirty pink sweater, even though the temperature had to be in the high eighties. The next thing she saw was a little girl chasing a pigeon. The third thing she saw was an incredible mosaic—a circle of white with the word "Imagine" written in the center with spokes of black-and-white patterns radiating from it. A faded rose lay near the edge closest to her.

"We're in Strawberry Fields," Ephram explained. "The mosaic's a tribute to John Lennon. You can see the apartment building he lived in right over there." He pointed. "Pretty much every day somebody leaves something. Like that flower. Sometimes it's a candle, or a poem. Even though it's been like twenty years since he died."

"Twenty-something years and people are still

thinking about him. Kinda makes that what-do-you-want-to-do-after-high-school question seem more important." Amy looked down at the rose. "Although you've got that pretty figured out."

"Right now, I just want to get in to Juilliard," Ephram said as they walked farther south.

"Yeah, but you want to get into Juilliard because you love the piano, and that's what you want to do with your life. I'm only thinking as far as getting into AP physics—since my dad has his heart set on it." Amy could hardly take in any details of the park. The difference between Ephram's visions for his future and her inability to see anything beyond simply graduating from high school was too distracting.

"You don't have to have everything decided right now. You know you want to go to college. Once you get in, you have a while to figure things out."

It was so weird to have Ephram pep-talking her about her future. She used to feel like she had a plan for everything—well, that she and her dad did. Now she was barely scraping by in a summer school chemistry class—a hard one, yeah, but one the old Amy would have aced.

"Now we go out of the park, and we're only a few blocks away from the picnic spot," Ephram announced. "Your problem is just that you're multi-talented, Amy," he continued as they reentered the stream of people hurrying down the sidewalk. "I'm only good at piano, so it makes it easy for me to decide what I should do."

"You don't have to try to make me feel better. I'm okay. You're right. I'll figure it out." Amy decided that the one thing she wanted to do was enjoy this weekend with Ephram. She only had one more day with him, then she'd throw all her effort into her chem class and figure out the big stuff later.

"I'm not trying to make you feel better." Ephram looped his arm around her shoulders. "I'm not the kind of guy who'd say I suck at everything but piano to make you feel better."

"You're exactly that kind of guy," Amy answered. "Hey, isn't that—" Her eyes swept over a group of white buildings, their massive arched windows glowing with golden light.

"Yep. That's Lincoln Center," Ephram answered. "We can eat our picnic by the fountain."

"Right by Juilliard, your school of the future." Amy hoped she'd be able to choke some of the food down while within feet of the place that would take Ephram away from her.

"Yes. But also by the Met, where we're going to see the New York City Ballet perform after we eat."

"We're going to the ballet?" She got another jolt of NYC caffeine—but it was carbonated this time, full of fizz and bubbles. She'd taken ballet since she was tiny, but the closest she'd ever come to seeing a real ballet was the *Nutcracker* in Denver.

But this . . . some of the best dancers in the world were in New York.

"Yep." Ephram pulled a pair of tickets out of his pocket. "Maybe someday you'll be up there, Ames."

Amy felt her eyes fill with tears. Ephram knew her so well. "This is the sweetest thing anybody's ever done for me." She couldn't think of any more words to show Ephram how she felt. So she kissed him.

The top of the Empire State Building was flooded in red, white, and blue light. The observation deck was bathed in patriotic color.

"They change the lights for holidays," Ephram explained. "All red for Valentine's. All green for St. Patrick's Day. St. Patrick's Day is big here. They even do all gold for the Oscars."

Amy laughed.

"What?" Ephram asked. "Oh. I should be wearing a blazer. I should be holding a microphone. I'm a dork."

"No, I'm just happy." Amy did a little pirouette. "This is all so amazing, this whole city, being here with you."

"I'm happy too. Who'd have thought it? Everwood's own Hamlet—"

"And Everwood's own pariah." Amy gave him a quick kiss.

"You can see my old apartment building from

here." Ephram led Amy over to the railing and pointed toward Central Park. "It's that one, the one that's a little taller. And if you count down the windows, the third one, that used to be my bedroom."

Amy's smile died. She slipped her hand into his. "I knew Everwood was a big change for you," she said. "But I didn't realize how big until now, until I actually saw it for myself." Amy stared out over the park. "You must really miss it."

"Sometimes I do, still," he admitted. "But I'm ready to go home." Ephram wrapped his arms around Amy's waist and buried his face in her hair.

"Home, huh?" she teased. "Meaning Ohio?"

"Yup." They both laughed.

"I mean it, though," he said, his voice growing more serious. "This has been a great weekend. But I would've been just as happy spending the weekend eating bad pizza with you and walking up and down Main Street in Everwood."

"Come on, Ephram. I didn't just see how big this place is. I saw how much of everything there is. How many choices you have. How many options at every second. It's like the city's alive and it injects you with energy. It's okay to say you'd rather be here with me than in Everwood with me."

"You know what, I never thought I'd be saying this, but there are some things I like more about Everwood. And that's with you out of the equation. Because with you in Everwood, Everwood is always going to win." He wrapped his hands around the metal rail of the observation deck and stared at the lights of the city. "You know that energy?" He glanced at Amy, and she nodded, totally focused on him. "It's great, but it's hard to actually think sometimes when you're in the grip of it. In Everwood, it's slower. And I think more. It's made me play better. Because I'm—I don't know—*still* sometimes."

"I knew just from this weekend that I wouldn't be able to take the buzz all the time," Amy admitted. "It's been great. But I feel like I've been on a caffeine drip."

"I'm not going to be sorry to get back to Connecticut. And I'm going to be really happy to get home where we can hang out every day. *You* made this weekend perfect, Amy. It wasn't New York."

"I wish I could be there for your final concert."

"I wish I could be there to bring you brain food and give you massages," Ephram answered, his voice quiet in the noise of the airport.

They'd already said many variations of the same sentiments, but Amy wanted to keep standing there, to keep hearing Ephram's voice, to stand so close to him that she could feel the heat of his body through her shirt.

"I know you're going to play the Tatum like no one ever has," she whispered.

Ephram snorted.

"I meant that in a good way!" Amy protested.

"And now that you know how obnoxious Zoe is, you won't have to worry about her, and you'll do great on your chem final."

Amy wished she felt as sure as Ephram sounded. Sitting in that midterm, she'd been hit with how deep her lack of understanding was. She had a lot of catching up to do, and the new stuff would keep building on facts she had supposedly already learned. "So, I guess I'll see you back at home." She couldn't put off leaving for the gate another minute.

"Yeah. Call me as soon as you get to school. I'll have my cell on me!"

She had to have one more kiss. Amy wrapped her arms around Ephram's neck, and let herself get lost in her last moment with him.

And then she heard her final boarding call.

She opened her eyes and took one long look into Ephram's. Then she forced herself to turn away. How was she going to survive the rest of the summer without him?

CHAPTER 8

"Ephram, I want you to reconsider playing the Bach," Ms. Kinney said the instant he stepped into the practice room on Monday. "This is the last point where you can change your mind. We still have a few weeks left before the final concert, and that gives us enough rehearsal time to really get in there and make the Bach your own."

"We decided this already." Ephram leaned his head back, and the tiny bones in his neck crackled. Even just sitting up straight for so many hours a day was becoming torture. Why couldn't they make piano benches with nice padded backs and lumbar support?

"Can you really tell me that you feel confident we won't have a repeat of the midterm recital?" she asked.

Kick to the nuts, Kinney, Ephram thought. But if

he was honest with himself, he wasn't sure he wouldn't butcher the Tatum again. His practice sessions were completely unpredictable. Sometimes it was like he was in some smoky club at four A.M., Fats Waller in the audience, Everett Barksdale on guitar, Slam Stewart on bass. Sometimes it was like he was in a Connecticut practice room—not jazz conducive. And sometimes it was like he was back on the observation deck with Amy. It made him feel jazz, but not play it all that well.

"What are you thinking?" Ms. Kinney prodded. She twisted her long, straw-blond hair into a knot. "Are you at least considering the Bach?"

Should he? He'd been playing classical much longer than jazz. If he got distracted up there on stage, he could probably pull a passable Bach out of his butt. He wouldn't make a fool of himself again. But he might not really impress anyone either. When he was on with the Tatum, he was *on.* He never lost himself that way with the Bach.

"Come on, Ephram. Talk to me. Somewhere along the line you ended up thinking of me as your adversary, but I'm not." Ms. Kinney sounded remarkably sincere.

Ephram studied her, thinking about what Zoe had said. Just because someone *seemed* conservative didn't mean they were. Maybe Ms. Kinney really was on his side.

"There are times when I think the Tatum's the best thing I've ever played," he told her.

"But not consistently. Is that it?"

Ephram swung around on the piano bench to face her. Maybe she could help him make this decision. "Yeah," he admitted. "I'm never sure which Tatum is going to come out of me. If I could control it, I would absolutely play it."

"Do you feel more control with the Bach?" Ms. Kinney asked.

"The boy's not playing any damn Bach," a voice boomed out. "Mechanical, boring, soul-deadening. That's what Bach is."

Will Cleveland stood in the doorway. Big and bulky, with the usual frown on his face. Ephram had no idea what he was doing there, but if he hadn't been sure Will would turn around and leave, he could have kissed him.

"Your father pestered me until I got on a plane," Will grumbled to Ephram. "Seemed to think you needed me."

Ephram nodded. He should've known his father had something to do with this. "Um, Ms. Kinney, this is Will Cleveland, my piano teacher from back home."

"You can leave now," Will told Ms. Kinney. "We have work to do—on the Tatum."

Amy found a cubby in the library and neatly laid out her chem book, lab book, notes, highlighter pens in three colors, Post-it notes in two colors, a box full of metal pointers to mark passages she didn't want to highlight, five sharpened pencils, one big pink eraser, four erasers to stick on the ends of her pencils, and a mini pencil sharpener with a plastic dome to hold the shavings. She'd binged on supplies after lab.

It's not going to help, she thought as she flipped open her notebook. There just wasn't enough time. She didn't want to admit it, but it was the truth. She'd picked up some facts here and there, but she didn't really understand enough of the larger concepts, and new ones—that she had no hope of comprehending since she didn't get the old ones—were being thrown at her every day.

Tears of desperation, self-pity, and just plain exhaustion threatened. *You are not going to be that girl crying in the library,* Amy told herself. She pulled her new day book out of her backpack. Maybe she *did* have enough time. Maybe she just needed to get up a few hours earlier every morning and review the old stuff, and then spend her nights doing homework and reviewing the new stuff. She started to sketch out a schedule. But seeing the amount of work on paper made her feel even more hopeless. She was drowning here. She wasn't going to make it.

Her cell rang. It would be Ephram. A little distraction. But when she glanced at the screen as she pushed the ACCEPT button, she saw the call was from her dad. Perfect. Was he turning psychic? She leaned deep into her cubby and softly said, "Hello."

"I wanted to check in with you," he said. "I know your final is getting close, and I wanted to make sure you're getting enough sleep."

"Not really," Amy admitted.

"I used to pull all-nighters myself, and they aren't the way to go."

They are if you have no other choice, she thought.

"Also, don't study to music. If you study to music, it's easier to retrieve the information while listening to the same music, and that won't be allowed, so it's better to study in silence. That way you'll be retrieving the information under the same circumstances you memorized it."

"Thanks, Dad." Amy hoped her desperation wasn't coming out in her voice. Eventually her father would find out that she hadn't been able to deal, but not tonight. *Please, not tonight,* she thought fervently.

"Is something wrong?"

Her father was so careful with her. He noticed the slightest change.

"I'm just . . . tired. Like you said, cramming, staying up too late. I'll go to bed early tonight." Amy cleared her throat. "So, how's Mom and Bright and everybody?"

"Oh, fine. Your brother's living at the pool. I just wanted to make sure you're doing all right."

"I'm fine," Amy lied.

"You know, if I have to say so myself, chemistry was one of my better subjects. I could come up. We could do one of the pretest tutorials."

"I'm fine." The lie sprung out of her mouth without thought.

"All right. Good night, sweetheart."

"Bye."

Amy kept holding the phone after they hung up. Not long ago, she used to tell her father everything. They had talked for hours about what college she'd attend, what classes she'd take, what careers she might pursue. And she had let him help her with her schoolwork when she needed it. Her father probably missed that Amy. Right now she did too. That Amy would be loving this whole chemistry challenge.

But that Amy didn't exist anymore.

"No, no, no!" Will barked.

And I was actually glad to see him, Ephram thought. After four days spent almost entirely in the practice room with the guy, Ephram pretty much never wanted to see Will again.

"Tell me why you want to play the Tatum."

"What's the point? I'm playing it." Ephram raked his hands over his head. "It's too late to play anything else."

"You want to try that again?"

Will had gotten quieter instead of louder, which meant he was about to explode. Ephram started serving up pieces of the speech he'd given the board. "I have a passion for the Tatum. You know that. And I want a school that respects that. If the Juilliard scout can't—"

"Bull. You have passion for something, but it's not the Tatum." Will gestured Ephram away from the piano with one jerk of his head, then sat down in his place. He began to play a one-handed version of Tatum's *Tea for Two,* starting out with the basic melody, then switching over to the arpeggios with all the flattened fifths and ninths. Even with one hand, he swung.

"Remember when you stunk up the room in Denver? Remember what I told you?" Will said, still playing.

"Basically that even though I was messed up over Madison, I could still use what I was feeling when I played. That the feelings didn't have to be good to work—just strong."

"From the mooncalf expression I keep seeing on your face, you've got some of the good to work with now," Will said.

Ephram considered that. *Amy.* Will was talking about Amy, and Ephram's feelings for her. Could he use them? Is that what his father had meant by learning to deal with distractions? Was it possible that he could think about Amy, long for Amy the way he always did . . . and somehow put all those feelings into his music?

He sat down on the bench next to Will and started playing with one hand, just adding the melody back in, nothing fancy.

Will actually smiled.

One day before the final. One free day. No class, no lab. But only one day. It wasn't enough time. Amy wasn't sure it was even enough time to pull another C. *Don't waste it,* she ordered herself. *That wouldn't be fair to Da—to anyone. Even if the situation is hopeless.*

There was a fast double knock at the door. Amy grabbed her wallet. She had ordered Chinese, not even wanting to take the time to walk over to the cafeteria. She pulled open the door and saw her father standing there. "I've got sandwiches, I've got a thermos of tea your aunt swears by, and I've got my *Intro to Chem* textbook, which is excellent," he announced. But he didn't step inside.

"I could use all that stuff." Amy opened the door wider. "My roommate has pretty much moved into the library for the day, so the place is ours."

"I don't have to stay. I can just drop this off." Her father studied her face intently.

Part of Amy wanted to leap at his offer—just grab the stuff, hug him, tell him thanks, and wave good-bye. Then she could tell him the bad news over the phone. Because it was going to be bad news. Whatever she was able to accomplish today would only determine the degree of badness.

But it wasn't as easy to pretend everything was fine when he was standing a few feet away, looking at her. "I could use your help, too," Amy admitted. The Chinese food delivery guy showed up, and she had a few minutes to figure out what she wanted to say to her father as she paid and opened the cartons.

"Dad," she began. Then she shoved a bite of lo mein into her mouth. She tried again after she swallowed. "Dad, I've been working hard this summer, I really have." It was true. She'd gotten distracted by Joel and by the Zoe thing, but she'd also put in a lot of hours. "But I was behind from the beginning. I know I was in chemistry this year. . . . Some of the stuff should have been at least sort of familiar." Amy shook her head.

"Then I guess we should start at the beginning. We'll get as far as we get." Her father opened his chem book. "'Chapter One: Names and Formulas.'"

"I'm okay there. And in chapter two."

He flipped to the next chapter. Amy stopped him.

"Okay, see, we're in the third chapter and there's already something I mess up on. I understand the balancing chemical formulas, but I don't always get the right answer on the chemical reaction stoichiometry problems."

"Amy, why didn't you tell me? I could have been helping you all along. Or at least we could have gotten started a few days earlier. I offered, remember?"

Amy sighed.

"I'm sorry," Dr. Abbott said quickly. "That wasn't helpful."

"No, it's okay." She shrugged. "I don't know why I didn't ask for help. I wasn't ready to be the screwup again. I thought I'd be able to start fixing everything this summer. But I just made it worse."

Her father rubbed his finger over the bridge of his nose. "It's not entirely your fault. I put you in this program without really considering if you were academically ready or not. I knew you'd missed a lot of class last semester, but . . ."

"But I'm smart, and I should have been able to—"

"No," her dad interrupted. "You can't be expected to leap ahead in a science program without the proper groundwork. Being smart isn't enough."

"It used to be enough," Amy said quietly.

Dr. Abbott nodded. "Well, now you're getting into more grown-up subjects. You can't float on your intelligence. You need to do the work."

"I didn't realize that," Amy told him. "I mean, when I was skipping classes and everything . . . I guess I always thought I could just jump back in whenever I wanted to. I didn't know I would get so far off track."

"You'll get back, Amy," he said, "as long as you're dedicated to making it happen."

She nodded. "I am."

"So let's get started. We'll do what we can do." He turned a page in the book. "Let's start with this problem. How would you attack—"

"Before we start, I just want to say something," she interrupted. "Thanks for coming."

"Without being asked?"

"Especially without being asked."

Ephram was back on that same piano bench. Back in front of the same audience. With the addition of Will, his dad, and representatives from the best music schools in the country.

He allowed his mind go to his New York weekend with Amy—burning their tongues on fresh slices at Original Ray's, trying to swing dance to a band outside Lincoln Center before the ballet, watching fireworks over the Hudson, kissing on the Staten Island ferry, standing high above the city on the Empire State Building's observation deck. Then he let go of the specifics and tried to hold on to the emotions, sending them straight into the Tatum.

His fingers danced, they raced up and down, they shimmied, they *played*, played with the keys.

Ephram was in the zone. Just him and the music. No, Amy was in there too, and so was everything he felt for her. Not just the fun they had together. And not just the physical stuff. It was the things they'd told each other. The times they'd been apart. The hurts. The secrets. The friendship. The love.

The passion of all kinds.

Ephram hit the last note. He didn't know what the audience had felt, but he'd lived the Tatum. He stood up, bowed, and spotted Will and his dad. They were both grinning. Ephram expected that from his father, but Will—Will was hard to please. Ephram shot them a nod and strode off the stage, the Tatum still hammering through him.

Amy raced across campus, her long hair flying out behind her. She bolted into the cafeteria, eyes scanning the tables. Her face broke into a smile when she saw him. "Dad!" she cried. "I got a B! In the lecture and practical!" She didn't care that she was on a college campus and that everyone could hear her yelling across the room to her father. She didn't care that everyone saw her dad hugging her. "All the B's should bring that C up enough to get me an overall B or maybe a B-minus for the class, so that means I'm in for the AP physics in the fall!"

"It wouldn't have mattered if you didn't," her father said. "I know how hard you worked. That means everything, honey. You're getting back on your feet."

"Just one more picture." Ephram's father pointed the camera at Ephram and Will. Will gave a low growl.

"Better make it quick," Ephram advised. "He's gonna blow."

The camera clicked. "One more."

"No." Will slapped Ephram on the back and headed toward the refreshments. Ms. Kinney immediately moved into his place, along with a tall, balding man who looked to be pushing seventy.

"Ephram, I'd like you to meet one of my colleagues from Juilliard, Mr. Edwin Krocker."

Ephram and his father exchanged a glance. Somehow Mr. Krocker did not look like a jazz fan.

"I insisted that Ms. Kinney bring me over to you first," Mr. Krocker exclaimed. "I loved what you did with that Art Tatum. And, to be frank, it was absolutely refreshing to hear it played at one of these things." He leaned closer to Ephram. "Sometimes I think if I have to hear another damn Bach sonata, I'll expire."

"Thanks very much." Ephram smiled at Ms. Kinney. To his astonishment, she smiled back.

"Was that your teacher?" Mr. Krocker asked, nodding at Will.

"Yes, he and Ms. Kinney," Ephram said.

"Well, they should both be proud of you." Mr. Krocker shook Ephram's hand. "I expect I'll be seeing you again, Mr. Brown," he said.

He and Ms. Kinney headed off to talk to some of her other students. Ephram's dad clapped him on the back. "I'm proud of you, son," he said.

"Yeah, looks like I have a shot at Juilliard after all."

"That's not what I mean," Dr. Brown said. "You've really grown up this summer, Ephram."

Ephram shrugged. "Doesn't feel like it. I feel like maybe I just got lucky today."

"Don't sell yourself short," his father said. "You came here to a place where you didn't know anyone and somehow you managed to stay true to yourself. You made an unpopular decision to play a jazz piece, and you stuck to it even when it wasn't going so well. And in the end, you won out. It was the right choice."

"Well, I don't think I would've pulled it off if you hadn't sent Will," Ephram said. "You supported my choice. Thank you."

His father beamed the ridiculous Dr. Brown smile. "See?" he said, messing up Ephram's hair. "You've grown up!"

CHAPTER 9

"Dad, can't you drive a little faster?" Ephram asked. "Amy's waiting!"

"Amy, Amy, Amy. Aren't you happy to see your sister and me?" his father protested.

"Yeah," Delia said, folding her arms over her chest and glaring at him from the backseat.

"Hey, I brought you three new baseball caps." All of which she was wearing, one on top of the other.

"I learned to do a backflip. Don't you want to see me?" Delia was still pulling her trademark pout.

"Absolutely. Tomorrow. I'll see it as many times as you can do it," Ephram vowed.

"I made casserole," his dad said.

"I'll eat some when I get home," Ephram promised him. "Just get me to Sal's. I saw Amy once this summer. Once. Do you understand?" If he didn't see her, touch her, within the next five minutes, he was sure it would cause physical damage.

His father actually slowed down. "I understand that you had a weekend with your girlfriend in New York City that was almost entirely father-financed, and now you expect to be driven directly from the airport to—"

"To Sal's. You'll see me plenty—after I go to Sal's." Ephram considered jumping out of the SUV and running.

His father chuckled—sadistic SOB—and then sped up. Three minutes later, Ephram was bursting through the doors of Sal's. Forty seconds later, he was kissing Amy, his hands tangled in her silky hair.

They finally pulled apart when the other people in the place started to applaud. And hoot. And whistle.

"So what do we do first? We have two weeks until school starts. What's the catching-up-on-summer-together plan?" Ephram asked.

"As of next week, anything you want," Amy answered. She looked kind of annoyed, now that he thought about it.

"What? What's happening *this* week?" Ephram stared at her.

"Family camping trip," she announced. "I just found out. We leave tomorrow and we'll be gone for a week."

• • •

"Dad."

"Amy."

"Remember how we talked about me making my own choices about guys?"

Amy's mother and father exchanged what they obviously thought was a stealthy glance across the breakfast table. Bright let a glob of raspberry jam fall onto the tablecloth.

"Yes," her father said slowly. He set down his coffee cup, as if preparing for a blow. The worry line between her mother's eyebrows deepened. Amy felt a pang of guilt. Her behavior had made them so paranoid.

"I just wondered if it would be okay to invite Ephram to go camping with us." Her mother instantly relaxed. Bright actually laughed.

"Oh, can she, Dad?" her brother begged. "I want to see Ephram in the woods, sleeping on the ground, attempting to chop something."

"This was supposed to be a family-only event. We haven't gotten to spend any time together this summer." Her father took a sip of his coffee. At least he wasn't afraid to handle china anymore. That was good.

"I haven't seen Ephram, either," she pointed out. "Not except that one weekend. We've been in separate states." Amy didn't want to push too hard. She didn't feel like she was in the position to ask for too much. But she couldn't help adding,

"It would be a chance for you to get to know him better."

"You say that as if it's a desirable thing," Dr. Abbott said.

"He's my boyfriend," Amy replied. "Wouldn't it be worse if you didn't know him at all?"

"I suppose," her father muttered.

"Is that a yes?" Amy half rose from her chair.

Her father glanced at her mother again. Her mother nodded. "It's a yes," her dad grumbled.

"Yes!" Bright cried. "Gotta get the camera."

Amy flew up the stairs to her room and dialed Ephram's number. "You're going with us," she blurted out as soon as he answered.

"Wait. Camping?"

"Yes, camping. My dad said it was okay."

Ephram hesitated. "But what about the part where he hates me?"

Amy flopped down on her bed. She hadn't thought she'd actually have to convince him. "He doesn't hate you. He's kind of like that with everybody. But, okay, maybe with you a little bit more. Anyway, he really did say you could come. And Bright will be there. And my mom. And me, of course."

"And this involves tents?"

"Come on, Ephram. You've slept in a tent before."

"Not with professionals. Only my dad—who is much more inept than I am."

"We're not *professionals,* Ephram."

"Do you own your own camping gear?"

"Of course," Amy said.

"Then you're professionals in my book. I, on the other hand, have retained my amateur status. At pretty much everything involving nature. I'll embarrass you."

"You will not," Amy said. "Nobody cares if you don't have experience. I promise."

"Has he ever put up a tent before?" Ephram heard Amy's father ask. Then he heard Bright click another damn photo. He was going to have to destroy that thing—as soon as he figured out how to put up the stupid tent.

"You wanna help me out here?" he asked Bright, his supposed friend.

"No way. This is much more satisfying," Bright replied. "Smile!" He clicked another picture.

"You do know water condenses on the ground in something we call dew?" Dr. Abbott called over from the campfire he, Mrs. Abbott, and Amy were gathered around. Their large family tent had been up for at least half an hour.

"Yes, I've heard of it." Ephram hoped he didn't sound quite as snotty as the good doctor, but he figured he probably did. Nice way to get Amy's dad to like him. He stared down at his tent and at the poles that were somehow supposed to hold it up. They looked way too long. Why couldn't this tent at least be like the one other tent he'd ever put together? That would have been somewhat helpful.

"I wasn't sure if you had," Dr. Abbot called back, "since you've decided not to use the ground cover."

Crap. Dr. Abbot was right. Ephram had laid the tent right on the ground, which meant it would go up with no ground cover underneath it, which would mean Ephram would be sleeping on grass and dirt with no protection.

"I'll get it," Amy offered.

"He can handle it," Dr. Abbott said. Clearly the tent had become a test of Ephram's manhood.

Ephram found the ground cover, spread it out, then moved the tent on top of it.

"He didn't check for rocks," Dr. Abbott muttered. *Screw it,* Ephram thought. If he had to sleep on rocks, he'd sleep on rocks. He wasn't going to move the ground cover *and* the tent. He studied the tent and poles. The tent had two thin sleeves that ran across it. Clearly the poles went through them. And the poles were too long because they bent, forming the dome of the tent!

He was getting it now. Ephram picked up one of the poles and gave it an experimental bend, trying not to show that that's what he was doing. Yeah, the pole was flexible. Good. He'd figured it out. Ephram threaded the first pole through one of the narrow sleeves. It went right through. He thought he heard Bright giggling, but it couldn't be about anything he was doing. Ephram was on a roll.

Before he bent the pole, he needed to have the grommets in the ground to anchor the poles. He was *definitely* on a roll. With the tent spread flat on the ground, it was easy to figure out where he needed to hammer the grommets in. "Do you guys have a hammer I can borrow?" he yelled to the Abbotts.

"This is the woods. You're lucky we brought tents. You're lucky we didn't make you forage for your dinner," Bright answered through a mouthful of hamburger.

"We're fishing tomorrow," Dr. Abbot said. "As for the hammer, you're an intelligent boy, Ephram. What do you think you could use?" He held up a bag of marshmallows and waved it. "These?" He cocked his head like a confused puppy. "You think about it."

Amy didn't say anything, but she did pick up a rock lying next to her. A rock. He would have gotten there. Ephram found his own rock and hammered the grommets in. He hammered so hard he buried the first one. He had to pull it out, and Bright got a picture. But Bright didn't manage to get a photo of Ephram hitting his thumb with the rock, so that was a plus.

Okay, grommets in, time for the tent pole, Ephram thought. The pole was light, easy to pick up by himself. But bending it and keeping it bent in the right position while trying to attach even one end to a grommet? Impossible.

"Houston, we have a problem," Bright called out, complete with astronaut crackling noises.

After what felt like a hundred attempts, Ephram realized that he had to attach one end of the pole to the grommet before he tried to bend it. The realization made him feel like a complete moron, especially when Dr. Abbott treated him to a round of extremely slow applause.

But shortly after that, the tent was up. Sweaty, red-faced, big-thumbed, torn-sleeved, Ephram rejoined the Abbotts. Bright threw another few pieces of wood on the campfire. "I saved you a burger," Amy said. She and her family had already finished roasting marshmallows.

"Thanks." He looked over at Dr. Abbott. "And thanks for inviting me along. This is great."

"Ephram, did you forget to stake your tent?" Mrs. Abbott asked.

He followed her gaze. His tent was gently bumping its way across the clearing. Dr. Abbott shook his head. Bright fell onto his back and kicked his legs, howling like he was raised in captivity. Amy raced after the tent.

"Excuse me." Ephram took off after Amy. With her help, he had the tent captured and anchored without injuring himself any further. He lifted the flap. "Come see my home. I'm sure you'll like what I've done with it."

"I like that you left the rocks. Interesting choice," Amy said as she crawled inside.

"A good decor should have contrast. Hard and soft. Light and dark." Ephram crawled in after her. Tent designed for one with the two of them inside. Sweet. Worth every moment of its torturous creation. Ephram stretched his body up against Amy's. She looped one of her legs over his. There really wasn't much space.

"Ahem."

Ephram jerked his head toward the sound. He could see a dim shadow outside the tent. A shadow belonging to Dr. Abbott. "Amy, have you perhaps forgotten the location of the family tent?"

Amy locked eyes with Ephram. "No." Her answer came out in a kind of a squeak.

"All evidence to the contrary," her father commented. His shadow didn't move away.

I thought I'd earn some points with Dr. Abbott this week, Ephram thought. *And I'm already in negative numbers.*

"It's been a long time since we've seen each other," Amy reminded her father as she followed him back to the family tent.

"So you thought you'd catch up by spending the night in his *tent*?"

"I wasn't spending the night. I know you saw me go in there. I'm not—" Then Amy got it. This wasn't a big, serious thing. This was just her father being her father, the way he would have been before. Before Tommy. Before Amy went to live with her grandmother. Before Amy took illegal drugs. Before the horribleness. This was just plain old dad outrage.

"Do you think this is funny?" he demanded, catching her smile.

"No, not at all."

Bright and her mother had disappeared inside the tent. Amy's father sat down next to the fire, and Amy joined him. "Has that boy ever been camping before?" Dr. Abbott jerked his chin toward Ephram's tent.

"With his father once, just overnight."

"Camping with Andy Brown. That explains a few things." Her father poked the fire with a stick.

"Ephram did grow up in Manhattan, you know. Not a lot of camping opportunities," Amy reminded him.

"He's lived here long enough to go plenty if he'd wanted to." Her father shot Amy a sidelong glance. "It tells me something about how he feels about you that he was willing to come out here just to spend time with you. He must have known I wouldn't be exactly . . ."

"Tolerant?" Amy suggested.

"Patient."

"So you think he cares about me?" Amy wanted to hear her father admit it.

"There are indicators," he said grudgingly, a small smile briefly appearing before he got it under control.

Ephram crept back to his tent after an early morning trip to relieve himself. He spotted Dr. Abbott heading out of the clearing with some fishing tackle. "Going to get that trout?" he called softly.

"Deductive reasoning. I like it," Amy's father answered, with his usual half-sneer.

"Can I come?" Bright would call him a total butt-kisser. Ephram wasn't opposed to the butt-kissing possibilities after last night's debacle, but he was also kind of curious about the whole fishing enterprise.

Dr. Abbott continued walking.

"I'm going to be eating; it's only fair I should help with the catching." Ephram fell into step behind Amy's father. Dr. Abbott ignored him, but Ephram refused to let that dissuade him. After about half an hour, he heard the sound of rushing water. Dr. Abbott stopped. "You don't seem to need to talk every second. That's good. Trout respond to noise and vibration—even if it's coming from land. They have good eyesight, too. So we're going to stay back from the bank as much as we can. And at first we're not going to do anything. Just watch. Get a sense of things."

"Like what?"

Dr. Abbott rolled his eyes. "Like where the trout are."

"Okay. I need some elaboration."

"Rings of water or a silver flash. Or actual fish rising to the surface."

"That last one I'd probably have figured out on my own."

Dr. Abbott raised one eyebrow. Clearly he wasn't a fan of sarcasm when it wasn't coming from him. "Amy doesn't care if you catch a fish or not. I would have thought you'd know her that well." He took off his watch and buttoned it into the top pocket of his fishing vest.

"Oh. You mean she doesn't want me to drag home dead animals and lay them at her feet?"

"No."

How did Dr. Abbott fill one word with so much sarcasm? Was there a course in that in medical school? "Are you saying you'd rather be out here alone?"

"I'm saying that if you're doing this for Amy or in a misguided attempt to impress me—"

"I thought it might be interesting," Ephram interrupted.

"The Manhattanite thought it would be interesting?" Dr. Abbott's cynical expression stayed on his face.

"Even though I can't put up a tent in under a minute"—Ephram ignored Dr. Abbott's snort—"I'm not a Manhattanite anymore—not entirely." His mind flashed to Zoe, with her big-city superiority.

Amy's father stared, as if trying to diagnose Ephram's particular brand of insanity. "I'm an Everwoodite, too, now," Ephram continued. "I don't think I could have played my jazz piece as well as I did if I'd never lived in Everwood. And not just because off Will Cleveland. Or Amy."

"Amy?" Without even looking at the guy, Ephram could see one of Dr. Abbott's eyebrows going up.

"Yeah, Amy. I used everything I've ever felt about Amy when I played at the concert at the end of the Juilliard program." Ephram forced himself to look at Dr. Abbott. It was almost impossible while saying something so personal about his daughter. "But, uh, I was talking about Everwood. Here, your mind can be still sometimes. In New York, there's this intensity all the time, even if you get so used to it, you forget it's there. I miss the rush, but being there for the weekend, I realized I don't want it all the time. I like having the stillness, the down time to actually look inside instead of outside. I guess that's what I meant about

Everwood changing the way I play. That inside stuff, that's what I tap into for my jazz."

"Take off your watch."

That's all Dr. Abbott had to say after Ephram spilled his guts? Ephram stared at him for a minute, then obeyed.

"The reflection alerts the fish," Dr. Abbott explained.

"Good to know."

Amy's dad stalked toward the stream, clearly expecting Ephram to follow. Ephram did, a thin line of light on the horizon indicating that sunrise was approaching.

Amy fed some twigs to the fire. *Where are they? They should be back by now,* she thought. She felt a hand gently rub her shoulder, then her mother sat down next to her and handed her a cup of tea. "Herbal," her mom said. "You seem stressed out enough. I'm sure your father and Ephram are doing fine—unless Ephram managed to catch Ole Hank."

Ole Hank. The trout her dad had been doing battle with for years. Dr. Abbott loved a good fight. Ephram had to know that; he'd seen her father in action. He'd be okay. *Why'd you have to go out there with him alone?* she thought. Ephram should have at least waited until he had her or Bright for backup before he tried to bond with her dad.

"Is it breakfast?" Bright poked his head out of the tent.

"Did you go help get breakfast?" Amy snapped at him.

"Did you?" Bright snapped back.

"No, but Ephram did."

Bright burst out of the tent. "Ephram went fishing with Dad? Alone?"

"Children, your father has never so much as gored someone with a fishing hook," their mother reminded them.

"He never went fishing with—," Bright began.

"Shh—I hear something," Amy interrupted.

"Two sets of footsteps. Good, good. I'm gonna get the camera." Bright ducked back into the tent.

Amy and her mother swung their heads toward the sound of the approaching people. Dr. Abbot and Ephram stepped into the clearing, carrying fish, and looking pleased with themselves.

Without thought, Amy was on her feet and running toward her boyfriend. It didn't even matter that he was carrying fish. She wrapped her arms around Ephram, knocking him back a few feet. "How'd it go? Are you okay?" she whispered in his ear.

"It was great!" Ephram answered in a normal voice. "I even managed to catch a trout—with your dad on net."

Amy scanned his face. He seemed sincere. "It was great?" she repeated.

"It's not one of the signs of the apocalypse, Amy," her father said dryly. "Ephram, fish. Bright will clean them."

Ephram handed Dr. Abbott the fish. Amy waited until her father had walked all the way over to the tent and she could hear Bright start complaining. Then she couldn't help herself from asking one more time, "So, it was great?"

"You know how we were talking on top of the Empire State Building about the rush of the city and the still of Everwood?" Amy nodded. "This was excellent still," Ephram said.

"With my dad?" Amy asked.

"Hard to believe, but yeah, with your dad."

Amy just smiled at him. Her boyfriend. Who had a good time with her father. Maybe her life was starting to come back together after all.

EPILOGUE

"Can you see?" Amy pulled her soft scarf a little tighter over Ephram's eyes.

"The answer is still no." Ephram felt her lean across him, then the seatbelt buckled into place across his waist and chest. A moment later, the car started to move. "So since this is a big surprise, I'm guessing that you won't be taking me to any of the places we've already gone this week," he said.

"Nope."

"Okay, that eliminates the swimming hole, Denver, Boulder, my house, Gino Chang's—"

"Are you trying to guess? It's not as fun if you guess."

Ephram didn't really care where they were going. What did it matter? He was with Amy. The only thing that could possibly be bad about the day was knowing that summer would be over tomorrow. "I don't have to guess. I've already figured it out. We're now heading southwest, after driving about a mile south."

Amy laughed. "If I dropped you off right here, you'd have no idea how to even get home."

"Probably not," Ephram admitted.

"Is that the Tatum you're playing?" Amy covered one of Ephram's hands with hers, and for the first time he realized his fingers had been twitching, playing a teeny version of the Tatum.

"Uh-huh. Sometimes now, when I'm feeling good, it'll just happen. I'm trying to get it to stop before school. I don't want a downgrade in my nickname." Ephram twisted his fingers around Amy's. "Or an add-on, even. Twitchy Ham. Not the way to start my senior year."

"I think it's cute."

"You're more twisted than I thought."

"Not the nickname. But the Tatum." They drove a few more miles, then Amy stopped the car. She unbuckled the seatbelt for him. It was something he could have done blindfolded, but he liked the contact, so he didn't protest. "One sec." Ephram heard Amy's door slam. A few seconds after that, she opened his door. "Okay, give me your foot."

"What?"

She tapped his knee. "Your foot. My hand."

Ephram did as he was told, trying to remember exactly how ripe his sneakers were as she pulled one off and replaced it with a hiking boot, then did the other foot.

"Okay, it's probably obvious, but we're at a hiking trail. It's kind of treacherous, but if you trust me, I know I can guide you up it. You trust me, right, Ephram?"

There was only one answer you could give your girlfriend to that one. But blindfolded hiking? That didn't sound like such a great idea. "Of course," he said.

Amy took Ephram by the hand and they slowly began walking up a trail that became steeper and steeper as they climbed. At first Ephram couldn't stop jerking his head back every few steps, sure he was about to bash his head into a tree. And when he wasn't doing that, he'd tilt his head down, as though it would keep him from losing his footing.

"I'm your eyes," Amy told him. "The path's pretty clear. But I'll move branches out of the way and I won't let you trip over anything."

Gradually, he got used to the new way of moving, and he started to become more aware of the sounds of the birds and the scolding of the squirrels, the smell of the pine trees and the almond soap Amy used sometimes. His fingers began to twitch, playing the Tatum. He forced them to be still, but let the music continue in his head—the music of passion, of his relationship with Amy.

"We're here." Amy lightly put her hands on Ephram's arms to stop him, then she guided him into a quarter turn and slid off his blindfold. The town of Everwood lay spread out beneath him. It was beautiful.

"The ski trail," he whispered.

"I drove around for a while so you wouldn't guess." Amy ran the scarf through her fingers. "This was kinda like our first date, remember? I brought you up here."

"Our first lunch together," Ephram agreed. He cupped her face in his hands and kissed her. "I definitely wanted to do this back then."

"It was more complicated for me," Amy answered. Ephram got that. Her boyfriend in a coma, and his dad probably the only doctor who could save him. "But there was something about you. . . ."

"The purple streak in my hair. My intense knowledge of manga," Ephram suggested.

"Your dark broodiness." Amy knocked his shoulder with hers. Her expression grew solemn as she stared down at the high school. "Last year . . ."

"This year will be different. We'll be together. Everything's changed." Ephram kissed her again, longer, harder, trying to infuse her with his confidence, with the love he'd had for her since that first day he saw her.

But as they pulled apart he couldn't help wondering what would happen after high school. He could end up at Juilliard. And he wanted that. He did. And who knew where Amy would decide to go to college? What if it was thousands of miles away from New York?

Would he really end up having only this one year with his dream girl?

EVERWOOD

Ephram Brown has a pretty good life in New York City—great friends, a gift for playing the piano, and a really cool mom. The only thing he doesn't have is the best relationship with his dad, famous neurosurgeon Dr. Andy Brown. How could he, when the Great Dr. Brown is too busy saving lives to spend any time with him?

Then Ephram's mom dies suddenly in a car accident. And as if things couldn't get any worse, his father loses his mind and decides to move the family to a tiny town in Colorado called Everwood.

In Everwood their new lives begin. . . .

Look for a new Everwood novel every other month!

PUBLISHED BY SIMON & SCHUSTER